# Lady Enigma

Una romanza giocoso e cianfrusaglioso

by
Veronica Verity

Author of *Romantic Resumes*
Edited by John Marriott, Ph.D. (Alberta) (Failed),
Author of *The Masks of Imogen and Desperado's Woman*

Order this book online at www.trafford.com
or email orders@trafford.com

Most Trafford titles are also available at major online book retailers.

Printed in the United States of America.

ISBN: 978-1-4269-7961-3 (sc)
ISBN: 978-1-4269-7962-0 (e)

Trafford rev. 07/16/2012

 www.trafford.com

North America & international
toll-free: 1 888 232 4444 (USA & Canada)
phone: 250 383 6864 ♦ fax: 812 355 4082

Readers attempting to make any kind of sense of this trash will be hanged, drawn and quartered.

The Directorate

TO. THE. ONLY. BEGETTER. OF.

THIS. ENSUING. NOVEL.

MR. J. H. ALL. HAPPINESS.

PROMISED.

BY.

OUR. EVER-LIVING. NOVELIST.

WISHETH.

THE. WELL-WISHING.

ADVENTURER. IN.

SETTING.

FORTH.

V. V.

# ACKNOWLEDGEMENT

The poems quoted from Sir Philip Sidney's sonnet cycle *Astrophil and Stella* and that from Edmund Spenser's *Amoretti* have been pil-fered in true Lady Enigma manner from *The Anchor Anthology of Sixteenth Century Verse*, Richard S. Sylvester, editor. Published in 1974 at Garden City, New York in the United States of America by Anchor/Doubleday.

# CHAPTER ONE

If you were to see me sliding down a rope from the roof of one of East Clintwood's most fashionable high rises to the balcony of one of its luxury apartments, you perhaps might mistake me for a character from a comic book, but if you were to take closer notice you would see that my costume has no cat's ears and my cowl covers my whole face. Indeed, the only exposed parts of me are my eyes. I am, however, in the same profession--if one can call it that--as the said comic book character, and like her I do wear a very close fitting cat suit and black gloves--without, however, extendible and retractable claws--but, for scaling walls, instead of boots, light, rubber shoes with treads. Unlike that person, however, I do not carry any kind of weapon--no whip or anything like that, and certainly not a gun; for, whatever the framers of the Constitution meant in Article Two by the right of citizens to bear arms, I am sure they did not intend to authorize their use in the commission of a felony--though I consider my cat burgling a hobby more than a felony. Instead, I rely on my skill in judo and karate. But like the aforementioned character's foe and frequent nemesis, I also wear about my slender waist what might be called a utility belt containing the tools of my trade.

On my way up to the roof, by the way, I had to use my skills in the martial arts. That episode does not really affect the story significantly, but it tells you something about me. I had come into the building--the security was no problem; in fact I'd worked out the lock combination long ago, and again, you'll learn later in the story how I'm able to do that sort of thing so easily--wearing thigh-length red stiletto heeled boots and a pair of fake glasses with my mink coat--a Christmas gift from my late father, not a theft--over my cat suit, the cowl pulled back and hidden by the collar and by my long blond wig, and carrying a large red leather shoulder bag containing my ropes and hooks. A man followed me through the door and across the foyer to the elevator. We entered together, and as I pushed the button for the twenty-second floor, he said, casually and with a smile, "Oh, my floor too." Then when the elevator door closed, he moved in on me--as I half suspected he would--and grabbed me.

Well, he made a big mistake, for, before one could say "Jozef Teodor Konrad Nalecz Korzeniowski"--as you can see, I have a bit of a literary bent--I stamped down hard with my stiletto heel on his foot, kneed him in the groin, broke his hold and rendered him senseless by applying my thumb and middle finger to the pressure points in his neck. I pulled his crumpled form into the corner of the elevator under the floor buttons and took a position immediately behind the door as the light for the eighteenth floor came on.

"Going down?" asked the couple when the door opened at their floor.

"No," I said. "Up."

"Oh, well, we'll wait."

I was lucky, but really, all I would have had to say was that I'd had to deal with a masher and was trained to do so. On the twenty-second floor, I got out and dragged my would-be assailant to the stair well and left him to fend for himself as I climbed the stairs to the twenty-fourth and highest floor from which I made my way to the roof where I removed and set aside my coat, boots and wig, pulled my cowl over my head, removed my belt and tools from my bag, affixed a light, strong rope to a convenient pipe, and lowered myself over the parapet for my descent.

How, you may ask, do I know where to find what I want to steal? I know because I have another alias and disguise, that of Madeleine de la Fontaine, French maid of impeccable standards and qualifications who cleans and tidies for the well-to-do owners of apartments, condos, penthouses and mansions, through which occupation I gain intimate knowledge of what is available and where.

So why do I slide down a rope from the roof to break into the apartment from the gallery when I could simply take what I want when I'm there as a maid? Well, in the first place, if I did so, my victims might become suspicious--and for that reason, too, I never commit a burglary on the night of the same day as I clean. That, too, would be suspicious. But the real truth is that cat burgling is not something I do from necessity, for I am quite well off, having been left independently wealthy by the terms of my father's will, but for excitement and because it is in my blood--as I will reveal more fully in a later chapter. Besides, you, Reader, want a few thrills, chills and spills in a novel of this kind.

I'm known among my underworld connection (whom I keep as few as possible) as Lady Enigma; hence the title of this playful and trashy novel--and that by the way, Reader, is the translation of the Italian on the title page--more or less; that is, it is more or less Italian. Veronica does not really know the language any more than she does any of the other languages she uses in her novels; she just uses a phrase book and a dictionary to crunch words together to look like Italian in order to appear sophisticated to impress the illiterate and unsophisticated.

Well, while I've been introducing myself, I have reached the balcony which gave me access to what I'd come for: the diamond jewelry and a few other objects of value contained in the wall safe hidden, not very

3

imaginatively, behind a very fine original painting--which I intend also to purloin.

And so, on the balcony of a sixteenth floor apartment I went to work to break in. Having fastened my rope to the balcony railing so that it would not flap in the breeze and swing out of reach, I drew my glass cutter from my belt and cut a neat round hole by the lock in the glass panel, reached in, unfastened the catch, slid the panel slowly and quietly aside, held my breath a moment, and then entered. I let out my breath, relieved that my earlier tampering with the alarm system had not been discovered. I then closed the glass panel quietly and tip-toed to the picture behind which the wall safe was hidden. Really, it would have been smarter for them to have installed it in their bedroom. That would have been a greater challenge to my professional prowess. This was really too easy. Quickly I opened the safe--the combination was no challenge at all--and emptied its contents into my bag, took the picture--luckily a small one, or I would not have attempted its theft on this occasion and by this means--from its hook and carefully slid it also into my bag.

Suddenly there was a sound from the bedroom down the all. I flattened myself against the wall and readied my hands for a quick strike. Someone entered the bathroom. I held my breath and stayed quiet. Whoever it was soon returned to bed, but still I remained quiet till I was sure all was well. (I'm glad I did not have to use force, for I rather like this couple.) Then I moved with cat-like tread--appropriate for a cat burglar--to the burglar alarm near the entrance to the apartment, disconnected it, turned the switch to "Off," for I had previously interchanged the wires so that when switched on it was off--and vice versa--reconnected the wires so that "On" was "On" and "Off" was "Off" again, but left it turned off, and abandoned the husband--poor fellow; he really doesn't deserve it--to his fate when his wife should reproach him for not having activated the alarm.

In a trice, I was again out on the balcony, and after closing the glass panel behind me--my mother taught me always close doors behind me when I went outside--I began my hand-over-hand ascent, the rubber treads of my shoes gripping the concrete face of the outer wall--and excellent way to stimulate the cardiovascular system. Very soon thereafter, the rich blond lady in the mink coat and red high-heeled boots descended from the roof to the twenty-fourth floor--in this line of work, one should never exactly repeat a pattern of behavior--noted in passing that her would-be molester had disappeared from the stairwell where she had dumped him, walked to the elevator, pushed the button, waited nonchalantly for it to ascend, entered on its arrival, descended to the lobby, exited the building, and, her stiletto heels clicking on the pavement, made her way down the avenue to a side street where she had parked her red Corvette and drove away.

I wonder what became of the guy I left unconscious on the stairwell, and whether he had a wife to whom he had to do a lot of explaining?

# CHAPTER TWO

I keep some, though not all, of the jewelry I steal, and I often wear it I when I go places where I know no one will recognize it; and many of the paintings and other objets d'art I put on display in my town house. It was a pretty good haul the other night. The jewelry was nice, but nothing I wanted for myself, though the pearls were tempting. On comparing them, however, with ones I already have, I concluded these were not so good, and I really have all the diamonds I need. What I really want are emeralds and rubies, but so far, for some reason, I've not been lucky. So a few nights after their theft, I am on my way to "fence" my ill-gotten--yes, I admit it--gains.

My fence has his establishment in a pretty rough area of East Clintwood along the Clintwood River, the hangout of all sorts of thieves and muggers. So far, however, I've had no trouble, and if ever I do, I think I can rely on my skills in the martial arts to deal with it.

I parked my Corvette in the dark alley behind Waterfront Street where my fence's premises are. Afterwards, I intend to spend some time at the Gemini Club--you'll know what that is if you've read Veronica's editor John Marriott's novel *The Masks of Imogen*--in which I make a brief appearance, but that comes later--but if you haven't, you'll discover in the final chapter what it is. I've been to the Club before with a date, and I've promised myself that, should I ever obtain my emeralds and rubies, I would appear there nude, one night wearing my rubies, another night my emeralds; but tonight, I thought I'd go alone in my "work clothes" to see what happens. Since no one has ever seen me in my costume, I won't be recognized for who and what I am. I'm wearing my alternate cowl--I do my own sewing; I was well brought up in the domestic virtues, and, though a liberated woman, I've never regretted it--with a small oval opening that reveals my full, red, beautifully glossed sensual lips--what other kind of lips would a romantic heroine have?--so that I can have a drink if someone should ask me--or should I feel like one on my own--or so that I could kiss anyone who might prove kissable, and as adornment to my catsuit, a wide red leather belt over my hips and a pair of red high heels with ankle straps. As a complement to my shoes and belt, I'm carrying a red handbag on a shoulder strap. Red and black make a dramatic combination, don't you think?

I locked my Corvette, activated the alarm, and walked across the alley to a door almost invisible in the shadows and tapped three taps three times--that is, nine taps in groups of three with silences between the groups. Got that? As you might expect, it's a signal. After a moment the door was opened by the ugly, miserable little one-eyed proprietor.

"Oh," he snarled. "It's you."

"Whom were you expecting?" I demanded sarcastically. "The President of the United States? The Queen of Great Britain? The Akound of Swat?"

"Very funny," he growled. "You know I have to be careful."

"Oh, you're careful all right," I snapped back at him, "you miserable, sniveling little weasel--careful not to pay what the goods brought to you are worth!"

"I operate this business for a profit, you know, just like every other business man."

"Oh, yes. And like every other businessman you want to buy cheap and sell dear."

"Why not? But what've you got for me this time?"

"You know I always bring you good stuff. Invite me in and I'll show you."

I pushed him aside and stepped across the threshold and dragged him over to the counter.

"You're all dressed up to night," he observed in an uncomplimentary tone. "Stepping out or something?"

"That's my business."

"You're always putting on airs with that costume of yours, thinking you're better than everybody else, never letting anybody see your face."

"And that's my business too."

"Yeah? Well, let's see your stuff."

I spread out my takings on the counter, and he examined them.

"Yeah," he said, "it's not bad stuff."

"Not bad!" I exploded. "It's first rate! I steal only from the best."

"Yeah, yeah. Ten grand"

"Fifteen, you miserable little twit! You can get at least twenty-five for this!"

"Yeah, well, you better know that Andreotti the crime boss has put his rate up. I pay through the nose to be able to operate this business for the benefit of the likes of you."

"Listen you," I said, grabbing him by the shirt front and lifting him off the floor--I also do body building exercises--though not enough to make me obscenely muscular; I still want, despite women's lib, to look feminine, because, after all, I'm the heroine of a trashy romance. "Andreotti's your problem, not mine," I said. "You probably make enough to pay him double what he wants anyway. I hear, by the way, that he has a new girl friend, a recent graduate of Princeton and a classical pianist. The last sort of woman I thought he'd go for."

"Yeah, yeah. So what? Just put me down. Twelve grand."

"Fifteen, or I'll smash up your shop and you with it."

"Thirteen."

I picked up a Ming vase from a shelf and held it aloft.

"It would be a shame if you had to pick up the pieces," I said. "Fifteen."

"Thirteen five--and keep the vase."

I really liked the vase. It was a very fine example of its kind, and thirteen five was actually a pretty good price, all things considered.

"Okay," I said. "Deal."

"Geez! What I go through dealing with you crooks!"

"You think fencing's not crooked?"

"I'm just a business man who provides a service," he said.

"That's what Al Capone said."

"Yeah? Well he was a pretty smart cookie."

"Not as smart as Lady Enigma. He got caught--and died of syphilis, neither of which I have any intention of doing."

"Okay. Okay. Who cares? So thirteen five and the vase. I got the money in the safe. Just a minute."

As he turned, I first set down the vase, placed one hand on the counter and sprang over it to place myself strategically beside him.

"Hey! What do you think you're doing?"

"Just taking reasonable precautions, Max."

"Geez! You don't trust nobody, do you?"

"I don't trust you, Max."

"I always give you a good price."

"After I've browbeaten it out of you."

"Yeah. Don't look at me while I work the combination."

"Max, I could open that primitive safe of yours before you could say Philippus Aurelius Theophrastus Bombastus Paracelsus von Hohenheim. (I also have a very good education.) Why don't you get a more up to date one from Devereux Security?"

"This one's good enough," he said as he twisted the dials.

He pulled open the door and reached in.

"Money's way at the back in a strong box," he said.

"Oh!" I exclaimed sarcastically. "Double security! An excellent idea!"

"And so's this!" he said, emerging from the safe with, as I expected and for which eventuality I was ready, a pistol in his hand. "Now we'll see who's--"

WHACK!

I gave him a lightning quick karate chop which sent the weapon crashing to the floor.

"You shouldn't have tried that, Max," I said.

"I--I--"

"I do not accept your apologies, Max."

A second blow to the back of his neck stretched him out on the floor of his shop.

"I'd have been happy with the thirteen five if you hadn't tried to be clever, Max," I said to his unconscious form, "but now I feel entitled to my original price."

So saying, I helped myself to fifteen thousand dollars from his hoard. As I had thought, he was very well able to meet my price and Andreotti's increased fees. I could have taken much more and he'd still have had enough, but I don't like to be greedy. I closed the safe and locked it for him. No point in being vindictive.

As I put the money in my handbag and tucked the vase under my arm, I heard from the lane my car alarm sounding. I rushed out of the shop to where three burly and ugly thugs armed with tire chains turned to face me.

My attire surprised them momentarily--just long enough for me to size up the situation and set the Ming vase safely to one side in a sheltered corner by Max's shop.

"Hey! It's Catwoman! Thought she was just a comic book character!"

"Nice set of wheels you got here, Kitty. Just toss over the keys and whatever you got in your purse, and there won't be no trouble."

"An' uncover yer kisser too, so we can have a good look at you. Who knows, mebbe we could all have a bit of fun together."

"Yeah," said the one who appeared to be the leader, advancing ing toward me, drawing his chain back and forth from hand to hand. "Shame to be all covered up on a nice night like..."

CRACK!

"Aa-aa-aah!"

My judo kick sent him sprawling, and before the others could react, I somersaulted between them and knocked them flying with a scissors kick. I landed on my feet, spun around and took a defensive stance with my hands at the ready. The leader of the group struggled to raise himself and come at me again, but a quick chop to the neck dropped him back on his face on the asphalt. I spun around again to face the other two, but they decided they'd had enough and hightailed it down the alley as fast as their dazed condition permitted. I retrieved the Ming vase, entered my car and drove away toward the Gemini Club.

An easy victory you say? Too easy, perhaps? You forget that I'm the heroine of this novel, and, as you yourself, the reader, always demand and expect, the heroine always wins.

But little did this heroine know what destiny had in store for her at the Gemini Club. That is, little did I know what would happen to me there.

# CHAPTER THREE

As I parted the curtain across the entrance way from the rotunda and walked down the few steps into the Gemini Club proper, one of the male members of a group of four young men--three of them casually dressed, the fourth in suit and tie--and three women showing a lot of decolletage said to the very ill at ease shy-looking, sandy-haired, brown-eyed fourth young man--the one in the suit--who seemed to be without a female partner, "Hey Philip! There's a woman for you!"

Philip! The name sent a strange and inexplicable thrill through my whole body! (You'll receive hints from time to time as to why I should feel that way, but you'll have to wait till the end of the novel for a full explanation, for at the time, in fact, I but dimly understood myself.) I turned to look more closely at the young man who bore the name. Quite good looking, but very shy. Was he what destiny had in store for me? A young man such as he was not quite the destiny I expected, yet I felt immediately, almost fatefully, drawn to him.

"I bet she's wearing that outfit to cover up the fact that she's a plain Jane," said one of the other members of his group.

"Yeah. bet she's ugly as sin," quoth a third.

"Sh--she has a nice fi--figure and--and very nice l--legs and eyes and l--l--lips," stammered Philip. "I--I bet she's pretty. M--maybe she's shy."

--Why thank you, Philip, I thought to myself, for coming to my defence! In fact, I am pretty--as noted, I'm the heroine of this novel, and heroines are alway s beautiful--but I'm certainly not shy. It's pretty clear you are, Philip, but speaking up in my defence shows you're not without a bit of spunk. I could almost love you for that!

"Hey Phil!" said one of the women. "You have a good eye, but I thought I'd never hear you say anything like that."

"Bet the figure's all latex and padding to fill out the catsuit," said her companion.

"Th--that's not very nice," Philip retorted.

--I began really to like the guy!

"Then why don't you ask her to dance or invite her to join you in a drink? I think by the way she's eyeing you that she's kind of interested."

"Oh--well--gosh--I don't think she'd--I mean--golly, I'm such a--a--I'm so shy and bumbly."

Shy of women obviously and probably made fun of all his life. Again, not quite what I looked for in a man, but maybe he just needs to be drawn out a bit. So why, I said to myself, don't I ask him for a dance?

I walked over to his table.

"Hey Phil!" said one of the women. "She's coming this way. Now's your chance. She might turn out to be the woman of your dreams."

"I don't know whether of not I am that, Philip," I said to him, "but I think that under your shyness you're okay." Then too the surprise of his friends, I held out my black gloved hand to him and asked, "Would you like to dance with a woman of mystery? The music's starting, in fact, just for us. So don't be shy, Philip. Come and dance with Lady Enigma."

"Oh--gee--gosh! Golly whiz, L--Lady Enigma! Th--thanks!"

"Wow! Hey Phil! Way to go!" called the people at his table.

"Are--are you masquerading as C--Ca--Catwoman," he asked as I led him onto the floor to dance, "since it says you can come to the Gemini Club as yourself or as the person you'd like to be?"

"That's the second time tonight someone's identified me with that comic book character, but my costume has no ears," I replied, as I put my arms about his neck to dance with him. He was only a little bit taller than I in my high heels so that our eyes were about level. I rather liked that. "I just like being a woman of mystery. As I said, I'm Lady Enigma. But," I continued, disguising the truth just a little in the kind of jest in which many a true word is spoken, "I must admit, in fact, that cat burgling does seem like an exciting sort of life."

"You--you look very--you look really--stunning dressed like--the way you are," he said.

"Why, thank you Philip. And you know, you're very handsome."

"Aw gee! Gosh!" He blushed a deep crimson. "I--nobody ever--golly! Th--thanks. But--but, I'm afraid I'm not a very good dancer," he said as he began to shuffle rather awkwardly with me as the music began.

"Get up on your toes more, Philip, and then just follow my lead," I said, "and don't hide your light under a bushel. I'm sure you have a lot going for you."

"I don't know. I'm awfully shy, especially wi--with w--wo-women. I'm not very macho."

"I can see that you're shy, Philip, but don't worry about machismo. It's just a pose--a facade--a cover-up--a bit like my costume. Macho men are all just muscle and libido and a lot of hot air and not much between the ears."

"M--maybe, but it's no fun being shy."

"I'm sure it's not. You don't have to be shy with me, Philip."

"Oh--gee--golly-gosh! It's so nice to meet someone who understands. Most people don't."

"Like your friends back there?" I said, nodding in the direction of the booth where we'd met.

"Yes. It was their idea to bring me here tonight. They're always trying to push me into doing things."

"Like dancing with a woman in a cowl and a catsuit?" I said with a playful smile. At least I think it was playful, for, of course, I couldn't see it.

"W--w--well, I don't think they actually expected we'd meet someone like you. I certainly never expected to meet anyone dressed like you."

"Does my costume bother you?"

"N--no. I--I think it helps. The--the waitresses em--embarrass me. They--they're t--t--to--topless."

"Yes, and I think that's exploitive. A woman should not have to expose herself unless she wants to--though perhaps some of these women do want to. Actually, some day, I'd like to come here nude."

"N--n--nude! W--with nothing on?"

"That is the usual meaning of nude, Philip. I'd probably wear high heels though, since I rather like them."

"Oh good heavens! Nude! I--I--I've always had this fantasy about going to a dance with a nice, ordinary sort of girl--kind of pretty, but she's n--n--naked and wears red high heels--like you--."

"Naked in red high heels?"

"Y-yes. Sort of kinky, I guess, but I like girls in high heels--and I like red."

"Philip, beneath your shyness you have hidden depths of sensuality!"

"Shy people have the same dreams as everyone else--or maybe even more bizarre ones--but they have a harder time realizing them. I don't suppose anyone could really have a date with a girl not wearing anything--except perhaps in trashy novels. Anyway, I--I'd probably be too embarrassed for anything like that. We shy people have fantasies about handling with aplomb situations that we really couldn't handle at all."

"I think you dream about escorting a nude woman to a dance because you need some excitement in your life, Philip. And some day, perhaps, I'd be happy to oblige."

"Oh! Golly! gee!" he exclaimed, blushing again, this time a deep vermilion. "A--anyway, d--dancing with you is exciting."

"Thank you, Philip. And you're catching on quite well," I said as we wheeled around the floor. "You're not such a bad dancer as you think; in fact, you're quite good." And he really was. "But you know, as one of your friends implied, I might be as ugly as sin under this cowl."

"I--I don't be--believe it. I--I think you are probably b--b--beautiful. D--don't ask me how I know. I just do. Y--you have nice eyes and--and l--l--lips."

"Thank you, Philip, for believing in me. But aren't you just a bit curious about me?"

(Maybe some day I'll show you who I am and what I look like, Philip, but Veronica wants me to remain incognito till the very end of the novel.)

"Yes--"Philip responded to what I'd said before the parenthesis, "but I--if you don't want--I mean if you want to--darn! I always get tongue-tied."

"That's all right, Philip. I understand what you're trying to say. You respect my right to be incognito."

"Y--yes."

"Thank you. But," I asked, my own curiosity greatly aroused and needing an answer, "may I ask what is your last name, Philip?"

"Oh--yes. S--sorry. I should have--"

"Only if you want to, Philip."

"No, I don't mind. It's Sidney--Philip Sidney--like the English poet."

Philip Sidney! Incredible! Why I should start so, you will learn in time, but I, too, as I said, at this time was only dimly aware of the reason.

All I can say is that now, suddenly, I felt confused, abashed, embarrassed and glad that my face was masked for I'm sure I was blushing a deep crimson.

"Th--that's amaz--incredi--remark--very interesting, Philip."

"Oh, I suppose anyone could have the name Philip Sidney purely by chance, but I'm told that in some sort of way I'm related."

"Is that so!" Again, I became strangely flustered, and to disguise the fact, I asked, "Do--do you like poetry?"

"I love poetry--and all literature. I--I wanted to study it at the university."

"Then why didn't you?"

"Oh, my parents said I should do something practical--so I studied Commerce. I work for a firm of accountants. The people I came with are all colleagues from work."

"But you're not happy in that kind of work?"

"No, not really--though it's all right, I guess"

"But not really satisfying? Philip, you should take control of your own life and do what you want."

"I--I'm saving up so I can go back to university and major in English."

"Good for you! Oh. The music has come to an end."

"Oh--yes. I guess I should go back to my friends--un--un--unless I could--might I buy you--a--a drink?" he asked as we left the dance floor.

"Why that's very nice of you, Philip. Thank you. I'd be happy to let you buy me a drink."

"Th--thank you for asking me to dance. I--I could never have asked you."

"But you've enjoyed it, I think, haven't you?"

"V--very much! Y--you're very nice."

"Why thank you, Philip. So are you. So why shouldn't we continue to dance together for the rest of the evening?"

"Oh--but maybe you'd--surely you'd rather--you'd like to--Perhaps there's someone--"

"No, there's not, Philip, and I'm very happy to dance with you--unless you don't like my company."

"No--I mean, yes--I mean--no I don't not like--I mean I do like--I just don't want to take you away from--Oh! There I go again getting everything all balled up!"

"Oh, Don't worry about that Philip," I said putting my arm in his and sidling up close to him, causing him to blush. "I understand your meaning. So, come on. Let's get that drink, and then we can find a table or a booth and talk. I enjoy talking with you."

"So do I--I mean I enjoy talking to you."

"Well then, that's settled," I said as we made our way to the bar. "Let's stay together--if I'm not being too bold."

"I--I'd like that. But I've been wondering what should I call you. You called yourself, Lady Enigma, but--but--I thought perhaps if you'd rather not tell me your real name--you wouldn't mind if I were to call you Stella," he said, "like the beloved woman in Sidney's Sonnet Cycle."

"Oh--"I exclaimed, rather taken aback. "Yes--I--I like that--Stella--Star--though dressed like this, all in black, I'm more like the night sky than like a star."

"Your--your eyes are like stars shining in the night."

"Why Philip! How poetic! Well, if I'm Stella, then I'll call you Astrophil. Star Lover and Star!"

"Y--yes. But," he asked as we made our way through the crowds toward the bar the bar, "why do you dress like you do--if--if I'm not being impertinent?"

"You're not being impertinent Philip," I reassured him with a smile. "I dress like this so that no one really knows whether I'm ugly or pretty to make the point that women--at least many women--want to be appreciated for more than just their physical beauty."

That, of course, is not my real reason, though it's a view with which I concur.

"Yes," Philip responded, "I understand that. I--I guess I sort of support feminist attitudes. A lot of the guys I work with don't."

"I'm glad to know you think that way, Philip," I said, smiling and giving his arm a squeeze, again causing him, to blush.

"I--I try to. I'm not sure I always act or think accordingly. It's hard to break away from what I've been brought up to believe--what society has conditioned me to think."

"What's bred in the bone--"

"Will out in the flesh--yes."

"Well, at least, unlike some men, you recognize the problem and are trying to deal with it."

But just then the bartender came up to us and asked, "What would youse like to drink Catwoman and guy in the suit?"

"Yes, Phil," I said, ignorng the insulting allusion to that comic book character. I'm getting used to it. "What shall we have to drink?"

"I--I thought m--maybe I might have a Scotch--on the rocks--if--if you don't mind."

"My goodness, Philip! You're really breaking loose, aren't you! And why should I mind, Philip--Astrophil? That's what I'd like too."

We placed our order and then, my arm in his, we walked with our drinks to a vacant table and sat down across from one another.

"T--to you, Stella," he said, raising his glass to me after.

"Oh! Why, thank you, Astrophil!" I responded, embarrassed, blushing under my cowl. At least I felt very hot, so I must have been.

We touched glasses and he put his to his mouth and began to drink.

"Be careful, Philip!" I exclaimed. "It's very strong!"

But too late. He'd already taken a gulp and immediately choked and began to gasp, cough and splutter.

"Oh!" he gasped."Oh gosh!"

People around started to laugh, but I rose and glared at them and went around to Philip and patted him on the back until the coughing stopped.

"Th--thanks, Stella," he barely whispered. "Th--that was really stupid of me. I'm sorry."

"No need to apologize, Philip. It's the sort of thing that happens all the time. I should have warned you sooner."

"It's not your fault, Stella."

"Well, let's not worry whose fault it was. Are you all right now, Philip?"

"Yes."

"Now, just sip it," I said and returned to my seat.

"Actually," he said when he took a sip, "it's rather nice."

"It is, isn't it. I'm glad you like it, Philip."

For a while we just looked into one another's eyes as we sipped our drinks.

"I--I feel a sort of strange magnetism drawing me to you, Stella," he said at last. "I--I don't understand it, but I certainly feel it."

My heart skipped a beat and my eyes must have widened to their fullest when he said that. Then I looked down. I'm anything but a shy person, but I felt that same strange embarrassment and confusion come over me again.

"I--it's strange, Astrophil," I said--I had called him Astrophil before I had even thought to do so--"but I also feel drawn to you in a way I can't quite understand either."

"You--you'll probably think I'm crazy because--because, even though I don't know who you are I have this strange notion that I've known you somewhere before--a long time ago--but I can't say when or where."

I reached across the table and placed my gloved hand on his.

"Astrophil," I said, again falling without reflection into the poet's name for himself in the sonnet cycle, "if you're crazy, then so am I, because I feel the same thing--that I also knew you once before--a long time ago. Yet--yet I'm sure I've never seen you prior to this evening."

"This is strange, it's passing strange."

"*Othello*," I said.

"*Othello?*"

"'It's passing strange'--except I think it's really 'twaspassing strange'-- it's from Shakespeare's *Othello*."

"Oh--yes--so it is. We seem to have very similar interests, Stella," he said his face brightening like the sky at dawn. "Do do you like classical music too?"

"More than anything, Philip!" I said, unconsciously reverting to his own name--well, of course, I was conscious of it after I'd done so; otherwise how could I be telling you of it?

"Gee!" he exclaimed eagerly. "M--m--maybe some evening you'd like to come and listen to some of my classical CDs?"

"I'd love to, Philip."

For a while we said nothing, again just sitting looking into each other's eyes, trying, at least on my part, and I think on his, to read there what it was that so strangely attracted us to each other.

When we'd finished our drinks, I asked, "Do you want to live really dangerously, Philip?"

"H--how's that?" he asked, his eyebrows rising. "D--doing what?"

"Playing the Blackjack table," I said.

"Oh my gosh!" he exclaimed, his eyes fairly popping from their sockets. "I--I've never played Blackjack--or ever gambled at all."

"Because Mommy and Daddy warned you against it?"

"Yes--sort of."

"Actually, if you're careful and don't get carried away and overreach yourself and push your luck, especially if you've had a winning streak, there's really nothing to be afraid of. Just be sure to quit while you're ahead. I'll teach you, if you'd like to try."

"Okay," he said, almost enthusiastically. "Yes. Sure. Let's."

We rose from the table, and I placed my gloved right hand in his ungloved left one and felt him shiver slightly. He blushed as before, but also as before, smiled shyly at me as we made our way hand in hand to the table.

"You really do crave excitement in your life, don't you, Philip?" I said.

"I--I guess maybe I do."

"Well, in this instance," I said as we approached the table, "don't let it get the better of you. First of all, of course, we have to buy some chips. Can you risk thirty dollars?"

"Oh, yes. I think so."

We purchased our chips and stepped up to the table.

"There," I said, "you have four five dollar chips and ten one dollar ones. You watch a hand or two first while I play and explain the game to you."

"Five dollar bets, Ladies and gentlemen," said the tuxedo-clad dealer.

"Okay, the dealer has decided to establish the bet this time. So, I'll place a five dollar chip on the table," I said, shoving my five dollar chip toward the centre of the table. "Now, he exposes the top card," I continued, as the dealer, after shuffling the deck, took the card from the top and showed it to the players, "and then places it face up at the bottom of the deck. It's called 'burning' the card, and when in subsequent play he comes to that card, he reshuffles the deck. Now," I said as the dealer began distributing cards to everyone who had placed a bet, "he deals a card face down to each player who takes a peek at it, and also deals one to himself. Now he deals one face up to each player and then also to himself. The point is that the player with twenty-one or nearer to it than the dealer's hand, wins his bet, and the dealer pays him and everyone else pays the dealer. Aces count either eleven or one, at the player's choice. Say you have two tens and an Ace, the Ace can count one, giving you twenty-one. Face cards are ten and everything else has its pip or face value. If your two dealt cards are much lower than twenty-one, then you can ask for another card--even two--by saying 'hit me,' but if you go over twenty-one then you've 'bust' and have to pay up," I explained as the game progressed. "But look!" I exclaimed, pointing. "That man over there has twenty-one on his first two cards--an Ace counting eleven and a ten-- that's called a 'natural' and the dealer pays him double and every one else pays the dealer," I said shoving my five dollar chip in the dealer's direction. "The dealer, you see has eighteen. He was best to stay with that. If he'd had sixteen or less, he could have dealt himself another card. If he'd gone bust, he'd have had to pay up. If he'd had a natural, there'd have been a tie, and no payments. Now, let's watch another round."

"You lost five dollars, Stella."

"You have to expect that. I may get a chance to win it back."

This time the dealer let us bet as we pleased. Then he said, "All bets doubled."

"He's feeling pretty sure of himself," I said, "and of course, in the long run, the house never loses."

Again the dealer distributed cards. His own upturned card was a King.

Discretely I showed Philip my cards. "You see," I whispered, "I have only nine--a five and a four--so in the hope of coming closer to twenty-one, I'll call 'hit me.' The dealer is not moving, so he must have over seventeen." When I'd received my third card, I peeked at it and said, "Oh! This is good!" I again showed it to Philip. "An Ace," I whispered. "Eleven--giving me twenty. Another card and I'd probably go bust, and unless someone else has twenty-one, I'll likely win--or at least tie the dealer."

And sure enough, the dealer, who had only nineteen, had to pay me.

"Now, Philip, do you want to try?"

"Oh! Yes!"

"Be careful, Philip. If you win, don't let your enthusiasm get the better of you. I'm staying out this time to keep an eye on you."

"Okay, but why should you stay out Stella? You won last time."

"I've done well on one play. Best not to push one's luck."

"Ten dollar bets, ladies and gentlemen," said the dealer.

"Oh-oh!" said Philip.

"You may still be okay, Philip. You can't avoid risk."

"No--I guess not."

He placed two five dollar chips on the table. When he'd received his first card, he peeked at it and showed me. A Ten.

"That's promising Philip," I said.

It was more than promising that his upturned card was an Ace!

"Gosh!" he exclaimed excitedly.

"Philip!" I whispered, also excitedly. "You have a natural!"

"I can hardly believe--Gee!"

The dealer had only eighteen and no one else had twenty-one and so he had to pay up to Philip.

"I think, Philip," I said after he'd received his payment, "since we've both done very well--recovered our money and then some on only a couple of plays, something that doesn't happen very often--that we should quit while we're ahead."

"If you say so--yes--I'm sure you're right, but gee!..."

"I know it's exciting, Philip, "I said, placing a restraining hand on his arm, "when you win like that, but don't push your luck. That's how people end up losing their shirts. Come on, there's the music again. Let's cash, and then maybe you'd like to dance again?"

"Oh, yes! I love to dance with you again, Stella--though I'm afraid I'm not very good."

"I think you dance very well, Philip. Stop putting yourself down."

"Maybe I dance well because you're such a good partner, Stella."

We cashed and walked to the dance floor, and as we danced, to my surprise and delight, he held me very close.

"You're overcoming some of your shyness, Philip."

"Oh--I--I guess I'm holding you too--I didn't even think--"

"I don"t mind in the least, Philip," I said, pressing even closer to him. "Hold me as close as you like."

"It--it's nice to--to hold a--a w--w--wo--woman in my arms like this-- especially a woman like you, Stella."

"You mean," I teased, "a woman in a black cowl and catsuit?"

"No. No. I mean a really nice, s--s--sexy woman like you. I--I've n-- n--never held anyone like you in my arms before--or any woman, for that matter."

"Oh Philip! You poor, shy soul!" I said, stroking his cheek. "But you don't need to be shy with me. I like being held by you." So saying, I lay my head on his shoulder. "You're a warmer, more passionate person than you think you are. Don't be afraid to let yourself be so."

"I--I--uh--I--gee--!"

"No need to talk, Philip. There are times when it's much more romantic to be silent, and now is one of them."

We danced in silence, holding each other very close, until the music stopped, and again, Philip asked, "W--would you like another drink, Stella?"

"Why Philip!" I teased. "You're turning into a lush!"

"I--I hope not."

"Of course you're not! I'm just teasing. I'd love another drink!"

Back at our table with our drinks I again sat gazing at him, overcome by a strange sort of happiness in his presence.

"You--you really do have beautiful eyes, Stella," he said.

"Oh! Why, thank you, Philip!"

"And--and very nice l--lips."

"Why Philip!" I exclaimed. "You sweetheart!" And I leaned across the table and kissed him on the mouth, making him turn a deep crimson.

"Oh my gosh!"

"Surely, Philip, that's not the first time you've been kissed?"

"Y--yes--except by my mother--and she didn't kiss me like you just did!"

"I should hope not! But oh Philip!" I said as I leaned back and reached across the table to put my hand on his. "My poor, shy reticent Philip! I assure you, Philip, it won't be the last time I'll kiss you--at least I hope not, because I--I want to go on seeing you--that is, if you'd like to go on seeing me."

"Oh gosh! Uh--Gee! I always say 'Oh gosh!'--wish I could think of something else--but--but--y--yes, I'd like to go on seeing you."

"I'm glad, Philip."

We sat staring into each other's eyes for quite some time, hardly touching our drinks. Then suddenly the band started to play Offenbach's "Can-Can" and the stage curtains parted and a line of eight cane-carrying women, all completely nude but for their G-strings, high heels and top hats, came high kicking onto the stage.

"Oh good heavens!" cried Philip. "They--they're all n--na--naked! This is probably why my friends brought me here. They said I'd see some i--i--interesting things."

"But didn't tell you what?"

"No. They--they probably wanted to embarrass me."

"Not very nice," I said. "No one should deliberately embarrass anyone."

"I--I guess I should try to--to experience as much of life as I can. I--I've never seen women n--n--n--naked--I should say nude since they're in public."

Just then one of his friends came over to our table.

"Hey Phil! What do you think? Are you enjoying this?"

"I--I'm enjoying being with Stella--with this lady," he said.

"Hey! What is this, Phil? This enigmatic lady sure must be having an effect on you! You've sure been dancing pretty darn close to her!"

"There are depths in Philip that you've never imagined," I said.

"It sure seems that way!" said his friend. "But hey, Phil. Though I hate to break up your hot and heavy tete-a-tete, we're leaving after this routine, so if you want to get home tonight--"

"I'll drive Philip home," I interrupted. "That is, if you'd like to stay here a little longer with me, Philip."

"Uh--gee! I--I don't want to put you out--"

"You're not putting me out, Philip," I said. And then I leaned across, and almost inaudibly so only he could hear I whispered, "Please stay."

"I--I--yes. That would be all right. I--I'd like to stay," he said turning to his friend.

"Well I'll be--! Geez, Phil!" said his friend, scratching his head in perplexity. "Okay! Okay! Holy--! Well! See you at the office on Monday."

"Oh Philip!" I said when his friend had left and again reached across to put my hand on his. "I'm so happy you'll stay!"

"Gee! Me too! Th--thank you--Stella. You're the most interesting--and nicest--thing--person--I've seen--met--here tonight. The nicest person I've ever met anywhere!"

"Why Philip! But, if you want, we can go now."

"I--I was hoping we might dance again."

"Then we'll dance again."

"Th--that is, if you don't mind, Stella?"

"I don't mind at all, Philip. I love to dance with you." After a few more minutes, the nude can-can dancers high-kicked their way off the stage, but before the band began to play dance music again, the stripper called Salome came on. I have to say that I found her quite impressive, and even Philip seemed quite taken by her performance--though neither of us was taken by the band's playing of Richard Strauss's "Dance of the Seven Veils." But I don't suppose anyone else in the audience was paying much notice to the music--or even knew what it was.

After that, we danced again, and the excitement of being close to him was almost more than I could bear.

"Maybe you'd like to go now, Philip," I whispered, rather seductively, I'm afraid, when the music had stopped, for I had but one desire, and that was to make love to him.

"All right," he said, quite readily, I thought.

"My car's outside," I said taking his hand and drawing him toward the exit and then, when we were outside, leading him across the parking lot toward my Corvette.

"I sh--should really be taking you home," he said. "It's what the man is supposed to do."

"Oh, it doesn't matter who takes whom any more, Philip. Women's Liberation has done away with all that nonsense. But if you like, you can drive. I don't mind. Here are my keys."

"Gosh!" he exclaimed, his eyes widening. "I--I've never driven a Corvette. You really want me to drive your Corvette?"

"Yes. Why not? It's no different from any other car--just flashier."

"Well--gee! Thanks! Wow! A Corvette! Me driving a Corvette!"

"You'll soon get used to it, Philip," I said. "After a while the thrill wears off."

He ran around to the passenger side, opened the door and held it for me.

"Thank you, Philip. You're a real gentleman--like your namesake."

"And like my mother taught me to be."

"Good people mothers. They get a rather bad press these days."

"There are mothers and mothers, I guess."

"Yes, that's true. But aren't you going to get in and drive?" I said as he stood there absentmindedly, seemingly in some other world.

"Oh--uh--yes--gee! I'm all excited and flustered."

"So am I, Philip."

"You--you are? You don't seem the type to be flustered."

"Well, excited at least. But come on; get in and let's be on our way."

When he had got in and started the car, he asked, "Uh--to--to my place?"

"We have to get you home, don't we, Philip?"

"Uh--yeah."

He put the car into gear and started off with a jerk.

"Oh! Sorry!"

"It's all right, Philip. Every car is different."

"It's not that. It's that I--I'm so flustered. N--nothing like this evening has ever happened to me before."

"Well Philip, to a nice guy like you, it's time it did."

"You--you're the first woman who ever said I was a nice guy."

"How sad, Philip!" I said as we left the parking lot and drove off through the deserted streets of the run-down part of town where the Gemini Club was located. "You're so shy you've never been able to get close to a woman, have you?"

"N--no. I'm sure not like my namesake in that regard. He wasn't shy. I'm glad you came along and found me, Stella."

"So am I, Philip. But," I reflected, "your namesake seems to have been too shy--or too stupid--to tell his love to Penelope Devereux."

Philip thought a moment, and the he said, "I don't think he realized he loved her until it was too late."

"I wonder why?"

"I don't know. Of course, it was a different time. Marriages were usually arranged in those days. People didn't go out on dates as we do today."

"That's true. Poor Penelope! She certainly did not want to marry Lord Rich."

"Though we don't know that it was because she loved Philip Sidney."

"True again, I guess, but I rather think she did. I like to think she did."

"I guess I do too--at least it's a sort of romantic thought--tragically romantic, I guess, especially since by the time he realized how he felt, he himself was married--so it had to be a sort of courtly, Neo-Platonic sort of love--well we just don't know how autobiographical the Sonnet Cycle is--but it seemed as though they were on the verge of consummating their love, but she backed off."

"You really know a lot about this, Philip," I said admiringly as we left the sleazy warehouse district to enter a residential area. "You should really be a professor of English Literature."

"It's what I'd like to be."

"Well," I said, laying my left hand on his right hand on the steering wheel, "as I said before, you should do what you want. So go for it."

"Yes--yes," he said, turning to smile at me shyly, "I really should, I guess."

"Indeed you should. But it's strange, if it really were true, that Penelope backed away from giving herself to Sidney, for she wasn't happy with Lord Rich. Eventually, though, she found happiness with Lord Blount."

"After Sidney was dead."

"Yes, I know. A sad, sad story--but finally with a happy ending for her."

"I feel very deeply for her, nevertheless, and you know, when I read the story, or tell it to some one, I feel--probably because of my name--almost personally involved--almost as though I was there."

--Oh Philip! Maybe you were there! Maybe I--but I must not give too much away at this stage of the novel. After all, I am Lady Enigma.

"Uh--here we are at my place," said Philip interrupting my reverie.

"Oh--yes."

He pulled the car over to the curb in front of a lowrise apartment block and turned off the engine and then just sat there without saying anything. Would he overcome his shyness and ask me in? I wanted more than anything else to be alone with him, and I felt that he wanted to be alone with me. I snuggled up to him.

"Th--thank you for--for letting me drive home in your car, Stella. Uh--I--uh--W--would you like to--to c--come in for coffee?" he asked. "E--e--except I think it's the woman who's supposed to ask the man when he takes her home."

"As I said, Philip, those old rules don't apply any more. And," I replied, leaning over to kiss him on the cheek, "I'd love to come in and see your apartment. Thank you."

"H--how will you get in?" he asked, blushing and with a perplexed look on his face.

"Through the door, Philip. How else?"

"B--but in your costume--?"

"It's late. No one's likely to see us. Or if anyone does, tell them I'm your cousin who's just been to a masquerade."

"I--I suppose that might work. Well then, let's go--I guess."

He ran around to my side and opened the door for me. As we walked to the entrance of his low rise apartment building, I again took his arm and leaned my head on his shoulder.

"Gee! Th--that's very nice, Stella."

"You're very nice, Philip--Astrophil."

We walked arm in arm to the entrance and entered the building. Philip led me down the stairs to the lower floor--have you ever noticed that there are no basements in such buildings?--and along the hallway. Before we reached his door, another door opened ahead of us and a woman in a shabby night gown and a bath robe stepped out. A look of shocked surprise came over her face, and she stared severely and rather disapprovingly at me and at Philip.

"H--hello, Mrs. Schultz," said Philip. "My--my cousin Stella here has just come from a costume party. She went as Catwoman."

That disreputable comic book character does have her uses, it seems.

"O-o-oh?" said Mrs, Schultz dubiously.

"Hello, Mrs. Schultz," I said. "Yes, I thought I'd pay cousin Phil a surprise visit--and he was surprised all right when I pulled up out front just now as he was arriving home. Wouldn't believe it was me at first."

"I--I soon recognized her voice," said Philip.

"Oh--I see," said Mrs. Schultz, somewhat dubiously. "Well, it's nice to meet you--I guess."

"Nice to meet you, Mrs. Schultz," I said, giving her my most winning smile.

"Yes, I'm sure," she said as she sidled past us. "I'm just going to dump the garbage in the chute. "

"Good-night, Mrs Schultz," said Philip.

"Yes. Good-night Mrs. Schultz," I echoed him. "Yes--I suppose so," responded Mrs. Schultz and hurried away.

"Is she always like that?" I asked as we arrived at Philip's apartment and he unlocked the door.

"More or less. I suppose she was taken a bit by surprise. Uh--it's just a little bachelor flat," he said as he ushered me in and snapped on the light.

"Why it's lovely, Philip!" I exclaimed as I looked about. The apartment was furnished with a chesterfield, a bed--Ah yes! A bed!--a table with two chairs and book cases and record cabinets and a braided rug. "You have some very nice pictures."

"They're only prints. The frames are worth more than the pictures."

"They're very good prints of very fine paintings," I said. "You've excellent taste. Oh! And look at the books and CDs! Oh Philip! Our tastes in reading and in music are very similar!" I exclaimed as I walked about examining his shelves. "But I'm being terribly nosy. Please excuse me. I just want to know all about you."

"That's all right, Stella," he said. "I don't mind."

I went to him and took him in my arms. He drew me very close and we kissed. (I'm glad I wore my other cowl that exposed my lips!)

"I--I suppose I should be m--m--making the coffee," he said.

"We don't really need coffee, do we, Philip?" I whispered seductively as I turned to put my arms about his neck. "Wouldn't you rather do something else?"

"S--s--something else?"

"You're holding me very close, Philip, and we danced very close, so I think I know what you'd like. I can feel it--if you don't mind my being so brazen as to say so."

"I--I--Oh! Gee! Golly gosh! I--I'm sorry."

"You're just normal, Philip--just human."

"I--I--yes, I suppose I am."

"Have you ever made love to a woman, Philip?"

"N--no."

I nodded toward the bed.

"Would you like to--to make love to me? Because--again forgive me for being so brazen--I dearly want to make love to you."

"Oh--! Gee--! Gosh--! I--I--!" "Don't be ashamed of your feelings, Philip. 'Gather ye rose buds while ye may./ Old Time is still a flying.'"

"Robert Herrick, but he didn't mean--"

"No, but does it matter?"

"N--no--but Andrew Marvel's 'To His Coy Mistress' might have been more appropriate."

"You really know literature, Philip. But let's not waste time discussing literature--some other time, maybe--But since you've mentioned Marvell, 'Let us sport us while we may' and 'roll all our strength and all/ Our sweetness up into one ball,' for 'At my back I always hear/ Time's winged chariot hurrying near' and it will be morning before we know it."

"You know literature pretty well yourself, Stella."

"We've a lot in common, Philip," I said, "but I'm not a coy mistress, and I think you'd like to do what the poem's speaker wanted."

"I--I--"

"Try to relax with me, Philip," I said, responding to his embarrassment. "I don't know why it is, but I feel very close to you. As we said at the Club, we felt we'd met before."

"Y--yes. I--I remember. It's strange. I--I'm sorry to be so shy, but I like being with you, Stella, and I feel more and more at ease with you--and I too feel I have known you a long time."

"Passing strange. So, if we're such old friends, Philip, what's to stop us from making love? You do want to, don't you?"

"Y--yes--I--I d--do--but--but--"

"Well then," I whispered, "no buts about it. So let's get undressed."

"Undr--! Oh--gosh! I--I've never b--b--been with a n--naked woman be--before."

"But you've seen a few tonight. This will be much nicer, so don't be embarrassed. But perhaps you'd feel more at ease with the lights out."

"Y--yes--m--m--maybe."

I walked over to the light switch, Philip following me with his eyes.

"You--you really do have such a lovely figure, Stella," he said.

"Why thank you Philip," I said turning toward him a moment before I flicked the switch and plunged the little apartment into darkness except for the sliver of light under the door from the hallway. The blinds and drapes shut out most of the light from outside. I turned my back to him and peeled off my gloves, unfastened the straps of my shoes and kicked them off, dropped my belt and slipped out of my costume and took from my handbag a red velvet mask of my own design and put it on to meet Veronica's wish that I remain incognito till the very end of the novel. Besides, as Manfred Andreotti told Imogen Edwards in Veronica's editor John Marriott's novel *The Masks of Imogen*, the mask she wore when they made love made her look sexy. Then before you could say Gaius Julius Caesar Octavianus Augustus, I returned to him and threw my arms about his neck.

"You--you look very s--sexy, Stella," he said.

There! You see!

"Why thank you, Philip!" I said. "Now, hold me. Hold me close!"

"Oh my gosh! Oh golly!" he exclaimed as his hands touched my bare flesh and then jumped back.

"Don't be shy. Don't be afraid to touch me, Philip," I said.

He hesitated a moment, then pressed me very close to him.

"You're so very strong, Philip!"

"I--I work out a fair bit, and I'm also trying to learn to box. I'm told it will help give me confidence--but I don't think it does, and I don't like it."

"Well, you don't need to be able to box tonight, Philip."

I began to unbutton his shirt and pulled the tails out of his trousers and then pressed my naked breasts against his chest.

"Oh--gee! Oh gosh! Golly whiz! I've never held a n-n-naked woman before. Oh my gosh!"

"Is it so terrible?" I asked.

"N--no--i--it's nice--exciting."

"And it's nice and exciting feeling your chest against my breasts, Philip," I said pushing his shirt away from his arms so that it fell to the floor. "Hold me, Philip, hold me again! Hold me tight!" I said.

Hesitantly he put his arms around me again and then pressed me to him.

"I feel very comfortable with you, Philip," I said and kissed him.

"I--I feel very comfortable with you, Stella--more, at least than I thought I would. I--I'm still embarrassed--a bit."

"Don't be, Philip," I said, "but you've got to take everything off too."

"Oh my gosh, Stella! Oh gosh !" he exclaimed.

"It's nothing to be upset about, Philip," I said as I unloosened his belt. "Surely you don't expect to make love with your clothes on."

Oh heavens! I'm so brazen, so predatory, but something keeps telling me that if I don't bring Philip out of himself--I feel he must be mine and I must be his.

"Oh gosh! I--I--"

"Come on, Philip," I said, stepping close to him and sliding my hands inside the top of his trousers, "if we're going to make love--"

"Y--y--yes," he said. "I--I--Oh gee whiz!"

Gingerly he removed the rest of his clothes, and I embraced him and pressed against him.

"Oh gee! Gosh! Golly whiz!" he exclaimed.

"Oh Philip!" I whispered.

"Stella! Stella! Th--this is like a--a d--dream come true, one I've had for a long time--but--but somehow it seems, even more, like a dream that I've been dreaming for--for longer than I can remember, like a dream from the past. I'm not sure what I mean exactly--I--I can't understand."

Dimly, only dimly--and it seemed so bizarre--I think I was beginning to understand.

"It is strange isn't it, Philip--but, as Hamlet said, 'There are more things in heaven and earth, Horatio, than are dreamt of in your philosophy'. But once again, this is not time to be literary--or philosophical. Let's just be who we are now, Philip, and make love."

"Y--yes," he said, and then to my surprise and delight, he lifted me into his arms and carried me to his bed over against the wall.

"Why Philip!" I exclaimed.

"Is--isn't this what the man is s--supposed to do?" he asked. "It--it's what they always do in the movies."

"As I said before, Philip, there are no rules, but it's nice to be carried just the same. I'm glad you did. And you really are very strong!"

Gently he laid me on the bed and then lay down beside me and we enfolded one another in our arms.

"Oh Philip!" I exclaimed.

"Oh Stella!"

\*   \*   \*   \*

"Oh Philip!" I exclaimed as he withdrew from me. "You're a wonderful lover!"

"I--I am?"

"Yes. If you hadn't been so shy and reticent, I'd never have believed it was your first time! You were great!"

"Th--thank you. S--so were you--so are you--great. I--I couldn't have done it without your help. I mean I sort of knew, but never having--"

"Oh Philip! You don't have to apologize. And if you're that good the first time, you'll be absolutely fabulous later on. But come, hold me in your arms. Oh!" I said as we snuggled into each another's embrace, "I'm so glad I found you, Philip--at last!"

"I--I'm glad you did too." He was silent for a moment, puzzled. "At last?" he queried. "That sounds as though you've been looking for me."

Oh--yes. Why did I say that? But--but it seemed as though some time, long, long ago I had lost--someone--him? Philip?--and that I had been looking and that now I had found him again. Yet how could that be, except--except--? But that seems so incredible. So all I said was, "I--I mean that I think I've been looking for someone like you for a long time, Philip."

"It's strange, for you see, I feel that I've been looking for--or perhaps better to say hoping that someone like you would--would come--along--"

"Oh Philip!" I said, "I think it's kismet--fate--destiny that has brought us together."

"Whatever it is, Stella, I'm glad it has, for it's wonderful--so wonderful I can hardly believe it."

"It does seem incredible, doesn't it--except that here we are, and we've made love."

"Yes--yes," he said, "and it's simply fabulous."

"Yes, Philip. Fabulous indeed."

I pressed as close to him as I could, and we soon fell asleep in each other's arms.

At least I must have, for the next thing of which I was conscious was of the dim glow of dawn just breaking outside the window of his apartment. Hurriedly I rose from the bed and resumed my costume. From my purse I took my lipstick and re-glossed my lips and then leaned over Philip and left the print of my lips on his forehead. From my handbag I took a kleenex and wrote on it in lipstick: "Philip! Thank you for a wonderful night! I'll be in touch! Stella."

Quietly I opened the door, looked to see that the coast was clear and slipped away down the hall and out into the empty street and to my car and drove away.

I arrived back at my town house hardly realizing I had driven there.

Something wonderful was happening, I know, something utterly, incredibly wonderful, something amazing, something astonishing, something that seemed impossible, fantastically impossible, and yet--

# Chapter Four

That night of my meeting Philip I was so excited I took a long time to get to sleep. It seemed that meeting him was changing my whole life. What was I to do? Cat burgling is in my blood--as I said, but you'll still have to wait a while to discover why. But could I remain a cat burglar and love Philip? Would he want to live his life united to a cat burglar--a criminal, really--though I never exactly thought of what I do as criminal--just as a sort of hobby. Most of what I take I fence and make anonymous donations to various charities. Sort of like Robin Hood, I rob the rich to give to the poor. I know, I know, that really doesn't justify what I do, but as I said, cat burgling's in my blood. And--well--there are still a few more items I want for my collection--as I said, emeralds and rubies, and a painting for a large space on my bedroom wall: a very modern abstract which hangs at the moment wrong side up--shows how much its nouveaux riches owners really care about art; for them it's just a status symbol--over the mantel in one of the luxury apartments where I work in my capacity as Madeleine de la Fontaine, French maid extraordinaire et par excellence--and I really do good work. How to get it is a real problem. But of that later.

Can I tell Philip what I do--what I am--to say nothing of who I am? I feel so badly that he hasn't even seen what I look like, but--but, as noted, I have to remain Lady Enigma until the end of the novel. All very silly, no doubt, but, after all, this is only a trashy novel and it's Veronica's idea, not mine. But then, for my own part, I sort of want Philip to love me without seeing me--I mean, what I told him was sort of true: I'm not just a pretty face--and to discover my identity on his own--and though it's probably unfair to expect him to love me first without knowing who I am--but--but if it is really true what I've begun to think and feel, then--then surely he must sooner or later come to realize that--that--

But, again, I mustn't tell--not yet--though maybe you've begun to figure it out--as I'm beginning to.

Anyway, for tonight I have a heist planned--or as that notorious comic book villainess-heroine whose name keeps turning up on these pages because of the similarity of our work clothes calls it, a caper. Tonight I'm after a jade statuette from the Sung Dynasty in a large mansion set in large grounds surrounded, like a military encampment or secret weapons site, by an electrified fence with a barbed wire overhang and patrolled by a pair of nasty Rottweilers. The owners can turn the whole security system on and off by remote control from outside; so if I were to deactivate it beforehand, they'd know something was wrong whenever they left or returned to the property. However, I *can* deactivate the system from outside with a little electronic digital device I've acquired--how I cannot tell you at this time; to find out you'll have to keep reading, which is what Veronica wants you to do, of course--but I can't deactivate the Rottweilers. So I'll have to resort to more traditional methods to get past the fence and avoid the motion lights.

Anyway, if I could just deactivate everything and nonchalantly walk in and commit my burglary and walk out again, it would be just too easy. How boring! Where'd be the fun? And where would be the excitement for you the Reader? The story needs a little excitement, after all.

Well anyway, I've got to come at everything from above, and therefore, the "caper" will have to take place very late at night. They've cut down all the trees on the edge of the property so no one can scale the fence that way--some people are really paranoid--but there's a telephone pole in the lane behind the property which I can climb and shoot a line with my crossbow across to a big tree near the house. Once I'm over the fence and on the roof of the house--a difficult and risky operation, but that's the fun of being a cat burglar--the actual burglary will be fairly simple, for then I can use my device to deactivate the system. I have a different plan for getting out--one that, as you will see, will cause the owners and the police to scratch their heads in bewilderment. Or at least I hope it will.

So at midnight I donned my costume and assembled my equipment--on this occasion I also carried a back pack--slipped into a pair of high heels--I like high heels, as I said before, and I don't mind pleasing Philip in that regard, and besides, I'm a Veronica Verity heroine--and a shiny black coat, and I activated my security system and drove off through certain half-deserted streets and dim retreats of one-night cheap hotels and saw-dust restaurants with oyster shells--I hope for Veronica's sake that T. S. Eliot's poetry is in the public domain, even though the quotation is not exact--to my destination where I parked in front of a garbage dumpster in the lane behind an apartment building. I slid out of my coat, pulled on my cowl, grabbed my back pack and stepped out. From the pack I took the parts of my crossbow and assembled it. To do so after I had climbed the pole would have been tricky. I then removed the bolt for my crossbow and stuck it into my belt, and took out a coil of nylon rope, one end of which I secured to the bolt, and prepared to ascend the pole by kicking off my high heels and replacing them with a pair of boots with cleats from my back pack, which I then slung on my back--where back packs are usually slung; that's why they call them back packs--and proceeded to climb the pole. When I had got as high up as possible, I first drove a spike into the pole, hanging on as I did so with my knees and the cleats of my boots--no easy task--and hung up my back pack. I then fastened the loose end of my rope around the telephone pole. I watched as the Rottweillers disappeared around the corner of the house, and then I inserted the bolt into my crossbow. Now came the really tough part. Grasping the pole with my knees and digging my cleats into the wood as hard as I could--Hey! rhyme and metre!--I put the crossbow to my shoulder, leaned out to one side and took aim and released the bolt.

THUNG!

I grabbed onto the telephone pole and watched as the bolt flew on its trajectory to lodge in the trunk of the tall tree at the corner of the house. A serious oversight on the part of the owners: they should have had that tree felled too. But I'm glad they didn't. It's a beautiful tree, and too many trees are cut down to satisfy our own selfish ends. (I'm concerned about the environment and make substantial donations--not just from the profits of my burglaries--to environmentalist groups to further their work.)

I gave the rope a tug to insure that it was secure. It was. Now for the really difficult part--to clamber along the rope across the lane and over the fence to the tree which was my access to the roof of the house. I resumed my back pack, and once more waited for the Rottweilers to cross the back yard and go around toward the front again before I grasped the rope in my gloved hands, kicked off from the telephone pole and dangled briefly over the lane before swinging my legs up to grasp the rope for extra security by crossing my ankles over it. Slowly, carefully, hand over hand, I made my way along the rope. As I got the feel of everything, I was able to move a bit faster, and soon I had crossed the fence. I reached around to my pack and unzipped a pouch from which I drew two large steaks containing tranquilizers which I tossed down to where the two patrolling Rottweilers would find them--a little more humane than darts from a tranquilizer gun. At least they would enjoy themselves before they passed out. My arms aching, I hung here waiting for them to trot into view, hoping they'd smell the steaks before they smelled me. After about a minute they appeared, and whether they sniffed me out or not, they found the steaks more interesting and began to wolf them down. The tranquilizer worked very quickly, and when the poor beasts had become somnolent and my hands were nearly numb, I resumed my journey along my rope until I reached the tree. With much relief, I clambered onto a branch and took a few moments to catch my breath, flex my hands to restore circulation and remove my cleated boots which I stowed once more in my back pack.

So far so good. Now to get into the house itself. From my back pack, which I secured by its straps to another branch just above me, I withdrew my little hand-held remote device. I had already discovered on my visits to the house as Madeleine de la Fontaine the programs for the security system, and I proceeded now to deactivate it. First the motion lights, then the alarm, then the fence. That done, I worked my crossbow bolt out of the tree, and shot it, with its attached rope, back out over the fence into the lane. "Though this be madness, yet is there method in it"--as you shall see. I don't want to leave any clues that might trace the operation back to me, after all. Then from my back pack I took another rope with a grappling hook at one end. After securing the other end to the tree, I edged gingerly along the branch until I had space, swung it in an arc like a pendulum a few times, and then cast it upward to catch onto the peak of the roof. As before, I tugged it to make sure it was secure, and then I began my climb to the roof.

Perched as I was now on the peak of the roof, I detached the grappling hook and let it fall to the ground where I'd retrieve it later. Now, I climbed down to the balcony below me. With my glass cutter, I removed a neat half-circle of glass from one of the sliding panels and reached in to disengage the lock. Quietly I slid the panel aside, entered, and slid the panel shut behind me.

I hope you've been able to follow all that, Reader.

So, there I was inside. Again, I took a deep breath in relief at having got that far. Now to get the statuette--and anything else of interest.

Oh dear! From downstairs in the living room where the statuette was located came the sounds of the television! Someone had stayed up and was watching it. Why on earth don't people go to bed in decent time? Well, that complicated matters, but I was sure I could handle the situation. I'd simply start upstairs with the safe in the master bedroom. I put on the night goggles I carried in my belt, tip-toed along the hall, turning off the night light as I passed, until I reached the bedroom door. I put my ear to the key hole and listened. Not a sound came from inside. Quietly, carefully, I tried the handle. It opened silently, and I slowly pushed open the door. I stood outside for a moment listening, and, hearing only the light breathing of the couple sleeping in the bed, I stealthily slipped in and gently closed the door behind me in case someone from the living room should come up the stairs. I tip-toed to the head of the bed, stopped, waited. The woman muttered something as she turned in her sleep. I waited till she was settled again and then carefully lifted from its hook the picture hanging above the bed to expose the safe. Again, I stood motionless holding the picture. No one stirred, and I gently set the picture on the floor. Again I paused. Now the husband stirred in his sleep. I waited. He settled himself and resumed his light, regular breathing. I placed my left hand on the head of the bed to steady myself, and with my right I unlocked the safe whose combination was really just too simple for an expert like me. Again, I paused to be sure no one had wakened, and then I took a folded up velvet bag from my belt and carefully, quietly placed in it the contents of the safe. Again I paused to listen. Nothing but regular breathing. Quietly I closed the safe, stepped back, paused to listen, and then stooped down to pick up the picture to replace it.

Just then the husband sat up with a start.

"W--?"

In a flash--metaphorically, of course--I let go of the picture--which fortunately I had not yet lifted--and grasped him behind the ears and applied pressure with my thumb and fourth finger. In an instant he slumped down unconscious. I stood silently trembling for a moment. It was a close call. Of course in a novel like this, one has to have one or two. I regained my self-control and steadied myself and then replaced the picture. Silently I returned to the door, listened for sounds in the hall and, hearing nothing, silently reopened the door, stealthily slipped back into the hall, and noiselessly reclosed the door. All was as if not a thing had happened. If you hadn't believed I was a professional, your doubts should now be dispelled.

I crept to the head of the stairs--stopping to turn the night light back on--and listened. Still the sound of the television. movies on the VCR. Did whoever it was plan to go on all night? Well, such are the hazards of cat burgling. I flattened myself against the wall and stealthily made my way down the stairs. Near the bottom, even though I knew that its viewers would not be facing my way because the television faced outward from the wall directly opposite the archway leading to the living room, I slipped quietly over the bannister and dropped silently to the carpeted floor to make absolutely certain I was not seen.

The movie seemed to be some kind of a comedy, and suddenly I heard two voices laughing, one male, one female. So the son of the household was in there with his girl friend. How, then, was I to get my statuette? Life can become very complicated at times.

I contemplated my options. I could go down into the cellar and throw the circuit breakers to the living room, but could I get back upstairs again before the son came down to investigate? Would I be on my way up again while he was on his way down on the same staircase? The other option was to sneak up behind the young couple--well, not really much younger than I--and render them temporarily unconscious by pressure behind the ears as I had done upstairs to the master of the house. I would have to be both silent and very quick. Well, I could be both. Then, quite unexpectedly, fate took a turn in my favor. From the literary point of view, of course, it's the intervention of the long arm of coincidence getting the heroine out of a jam. Writers are often taken to task for employing it, but to give Veronica credit, she does not overuse it. And coincidences do happen, after all. So, Reader, don't be too critical.

The coincidence here was that the movie ended, and the young couple became more interested in each other--as one would expect to happen eventually--Note that I do not split infinitives; at least, Veronica doesn't--in such circumstances than in watching another one. Perhaps, of course, they didn't have another movie. Either way, eventually was now, and it worked to my advantage. Heads fell below the back of the sofa and then an arm rose above it and turned out the light--which was helpful, but I felt rather like a voyeur or a trespasser; so I won't repeat anything I heard--it was the usual sort of silly things that are said in such circumstances--and I vowed not to look as I purloined the statuette which stood on a pedestal in the corner of the room. With cat-like tread--due acknowledgement to Gilbert and Sullivan--I entered the living room stealthily, crouched low and silently made my way over to the table. I admit that, as a precaution, I had to cast an occasional glance in the direction of the sofa, but I kept them brief. Within moments I reached the table and carefully, very carefully, lifted the statuette from its base and stealthily--how else should one move when one is stealing?--I passed from the living room into the adjacent dining room and thence to the kitchen where I carefully wrapped the statuette in a velvet cloth I had brought with me for the purpose and placed it into my bag.

It suddenly occurred to me that with all the delays, the Rottweilers might be waking from their stupor. I had given them only enough tranquilizer to keep them unconscious for what I thought would be sufficient time for me to do my job and get away. If they were awake when I left the house the whole enterprise would come to naught. I had to think quickly. Ah! The refrigerator! Very carefully so as to make no noise I opened the door and slid open the meat keeper. Steaks! Several of them and big ones! (Coincident again, but one expects to find meat in a meat of some kind keeper, after all.) I grabbed four of them, closed the refrigerator quietly and proceeded to the back door. In a moment I was outside.

Yes, as I had feared, the Rottweillers were beginning to regain consciousness, but not yet completely. I hoped I had time to climb the tree, unfasten my rope, return to the ground and pick up my grappling hook before they were fully alert. If not, I hoped the steaks would keep them occupied while I finished my business. Quickly I scaled the tree. (I've been climbing trees since I was a kid, so that was a piece of cake.) Equally quickly, I untied my rope and began the descent. When I was half way down, one of the Rottweillers grumbled--not growled, not yet, but he gave me sufficient warning that I had to be quick. I scurried over to my grappling hook and, just as I bent to take it up, the other Rottweiller growled. Very definitely growled this time. Judging the distance and the effort carefully, I tossed two steaks to land just under their noses and ran as silently and as quickly as possible to the fence. Taking a pair of wire cutters from my belt, I cut an opening in the chain-link fence, ran to my car, pulled the line attached to the bolt of my crossbow away from the fence and with my pocket computer, reactivated the house security system. Quickly I gathered up all my equipment, turned off the security alarm on my car--I forgot to mention that I'd activated it, but by now you should take it for granted that I always do--got in and drove away. Whew! A bit of a close shave, but I enjoyed the excitement. I hope it met with your approval, Reader.

Tomorrow when they miss their statuette and call the police, they'll all wonder how on earth a thief could have cut through an electrified fence and entered a house with an activated security system. The company that sold them the system will probably get an angry phone call. I feel a bit guilty, because it really is a good system. It's just that they reckoned without Lady Enigma. The system hasn't been designed yet that can foil her--me.

Oh yes. I barbecued the other two steaks, one each, the next night and the night after. They were delicious!

# CHAPTER FIVE

The carved jade statuette looks very well in the little niche on the landing at the turn of the stairs to the second floor of my town house--the first floor if you're an English reader. About the rest of my takings, I was somewhat disappointed--not that it was not good stuff that would bring a good price when I fenced it, but because I still hadn't got my rubies or emeralds. Tonight, after I had fenced my takings, I would meet Philip at the Club. As before, I parked my Corvette in the dingy lane opposite the dark doorway to my fence's establishment. Before locking the car and setting the security alarm, I dragged from the back seat a store mannequin I had found at a sleazy pawn shop and had painted black so that in the dark it would look like me in my costume. After my last experience with Max I was suspicious of what he might try to do in revenge. I noticed as I reached the door that he had installed a peep hole so he could see who was outside knocking. I had a pretty good notion why he wanted to.

I set up my mannequin so he could see it through the peep hole, tapped out my usual signal, stepped aside so that I would be out of sight when it opened, and waited. After a few moments I heard Max's shuffle as he approached the door. There was a brief pause, and then the sound of three shots as three bullets smashed through the door and into my mannequin, sending it crashing to the ground. Again a pause and then the door opened cautiously, and Max's hand appeared holding a smoking revolver. I waited until, as I expected, he fired an insurance bullet into my poor unfortunate mannequin.

"There!" he snarled. "That'll teach you to..."

WHACK!

Before he could finish what he intended to say, with a blow of the edge of my hand to the wrist, I knocked his weapon to the ground, and on the instant sprang into the doorway, grabbed him by the wrist and before you could say Pablo Martin Meliton de Sarasate y Navascues--I'm also, as I told Philip, a lover of classical music--spun about, knocked him off balance with my hip and flung him over my shoulder and laid him out flat on his back on the ground.

"That'll teach me what, you miserable little snit!" I snapped.

His only response was a groan.

I reached down, picked up his revolver and dropped it into my bag and then grabbed the lapels of his grubby jacket, yanked him to his feet and gave him a good shaking.

"I thought you'd try something like that, you sniveling, cretinous creep! I ought to wring your scrawny, scrofulous neck! With whom do you think you're dealing, anyway!"

Even in moments of intense anger I remember to speak grammatically: "with whom," not "with who."

Trembling, teeth chattering, he stammered, "I--I--I--"

"Yes? "Yes?" I demanded. "You what!"

Again all he could do was stammer, "I--I--I--You--you--you--"

Well, at least that was some slight variation on his first utterance.

"My, aren't we articulate tonight! Get inside, you blackguard!" I said and pushed him into his shop. I propelled him down the hall and shoved him into his chair behind the counter, stepped over to the drawer, scooped out all the money it contained--without counting it I could tell by the size of the bills it was a considerable amount--and emptied my bag of takings from the night before on the counter.

"That should cover it," I said. "And don't you ever try a stunt like that again, or it will be the last thing you ever do! I'll blow the whistle on you to Andreotti."

"I--I gotta pay him tomorrow, and you've cleaned me out," he whimpered.

"You've got my stuff, and I'm sure you have money socked away in your safe--and I see you took my advice and got one of Devereux Security's better models. You're not exactly running a charity, so you'll manage. Meanwhile, I hope you've learned a lesson--not to play games with Lady Enigma!"

As I turned to go, I noticed a fine piece of cloisonne work. As I stowed it in my bag, I said, "I'll take this as compensation for my mannequin that you shot up--and for all the extra strain you put me to tonight."

On reaching the door, I decided it might be well if I were to look out through the peep hole. And it was well I did, for as I half expected, the goons were back, and in greater force this time. Well, I was ready. I snapped open my hand bag and felt in it for the little canister of mace I always carry in case of just such emergencies.

"Come out, Girly," said one of the goons, the one who had wielded the chain on the previous occasion. Today he had a crowbar, as did his companions. "We know you're in there, and if you don't come out to us, we'll come in after you."

"Yeah," said one of the others. "We wanna see what you look like under that Catwoman costume."

Another reference to that reprobate comic book character! Really! If for nothing else they deserved everything they were going to get. So let them come! I yanked open the door.

"Come and get me if you think you can!" I taunted them as I stepped out."

They advanced menacingly toward me. Unlike that Canadian police officer I saw on television pepper spraying peaceful student protesters at the University of British Columbia in Vancouver to protect, so they said, Asian dictators during the Asia Pacific Economic Conference--I'd always thought Canada was a democracy--I let my adversaries make the first move and waited until they were almost on me before I let them have it with the mace. I was, nevertheless, as liberal with it as the policeman and his cohorts but on much more deserving recipients.

Crowbars fell with a clatter to the surface of the lane, hands went up to eyes, and tongues cried out in agony.

"Oh!"

"Ow!"

"Help!"

"Yih!"

"A--a-ah!"

"The bloody bitch!"

He who uttered that last remark slumped to the ground after I delivered a karate chop to his windpipe. Others swung or kicked out blindly, but my judo and karate skills soon laid them to the ground.

"That will teach you to fool with Lady Enigma!" I said as I stepped over their prostrate forms to get to my Corvette. After disengaging the security alarm and the steering wheel club, I drove away. I tossed Max's revolver into the Clintwood River as I drove past and went to meet Philip for our date at the Gemini Club.

The things Veronica puts me through to make this novel exciting! I could really have done quite nicely without all that shilly-shallying at Max's place. It's made me late. I hope Philip hasn't grown impatient waiting for me. It often falls out that a cat burglar's lot, like a policeman's, is not a happy one.

# Chapter Six

Philip, looking a bit anxious, was waiting outside his apartment building when I drove up.

"Oh Philip!" I apologized as I opened the passenger door for him to get in. "I'm sorry I'm late!"

"You're not late, Stella," he said.

"I am late, Philip. Don't be kind when I don't deserve it."

"'Treat a man'--or a woman--'as he'--or she--'deserves, and who shall 'scape whipping.'"

"Hamlet. Yes, all right, true enough, but don't deny that I am late."

"All right, but not very. If--if," he stammered, blushing a deep crimson, "you--you give me a--a kiss, I'll forgive you."

His smile was shy, but there was a hint of teasing in it which I liked.

"Oh Philip! You're sweet. I'd love to give you a kiss," I said and leaned over to kiss him on the lips. "There--that's to apologize for being late. And this," I said, kissing him again, "is for being so sweet about it, and this," I said kissing him yet again, "is for being Philip and because I like to kiss you."

"Oh Stella!" he exclaimed.

"My goodness. You can be as late as often as you want if this is what happens!"

"You know, Philip, I think you're starting to come out of yourself."

"If I am, it's thanks to you, Stella."

"Oh dear! Before this becomes a meeting of the East Clintwood Mutual Admiration Society, I think we'd better be off to the Gemini Club."

"Be--before we do," he said, "I--I got this for you."

He held out to me a celluloid-covered box containing a corsage of red roses.

"Why Philip! It's lovely!" I cried. "This will the first time this outfit's been graced with a corsage. Will you pin it on for me?"

"Oh--a--all right. Gee whiz! I--I hope I don't stick the pin into you."

With slightly trembling hands he pinned the corsage just below the left shoulder of my costume and above my left breast.

"There," he said, sitting back to look at the result of his handy work.

"And you didn't stick me. Thank you Philip. It really is lovely. But let's be on our way."

"Yes."

And without further ado, I put the Corvette into drive, and off we went.

"I still don't know why you like me, Stella," Philip said as we passed from suburbia into the dingy streets of the warehouse district where the Gemini Club was located.

"Why Philip? Why shouldn't I like you?"

"Well, I'm so sort of diffident and shy and gauche--not macho--and you're so full of self-confidence."

"Oh Philip! Macho men, as I said before, are a pain in the neck. Besides, I think my attraction to you has some origin beyond me and beyond you--that it's somehow fated or predetermined--predestined--I don't know what's the right word--and I believe that there's a much stronger man within you than appears on the surface and who just needs drawing out, and somehow--and I hope I don't sound arrogant--I think I've been sent to you to do that--and that you've been sent to me for a reason I can't yet fathom--but maybe to draw out that stronger man".

He was silent some moments and sat looking intently at me.

"It--it's funny," he said at last, "but I have rather similar feelings--at least that you've been sent to me. As yet I can't see any reason why I've been sent to you."

"I--I think," I said, furrowing my brow, though invisibly so under my cowl, "maybe it has something to do with--with--I can't say with what yet, Philip. It's complicated. I'll understand, I think when the time comes to tell you who--and what--I am."

"Now I'm even more mystified than ever," he sighed.

"Oh Philip!" I said, taking my right hand off the steering wheel to touch his knee, "I'm sorry to be so mysterious. I promise you, I will reveal everything to you soon."

"I look forward to that, Stella," he said, after some hesitation placing his hand on mine, "but for now it's fun having a mysterious, enigmatic girl friend."

"It's kind and gracious of you to say that because I feel that I'm being terribly mean to you."

"You're not being mean, Stella. I'm sure you have your reasons."

"I hope," I said apprehensively, "you won't be upset when you find out what they are."

"You're the best thing that has ever happened to me. Whatever they are, I'll stick by you."

"Oh Philip!" I said, giving his hand a squeeze. "You sweetheart! But," I said, one-handedly wheeling the Corvette into the parking lot, "here we are at the Gemini Club."

We got out and walked to the Club, I placing my arm in his and leaning my head on his shoulder.

"That's nice, Stella," he said.

When we reached the entrance he opened the door and held it for me to precede him into the rotunda. "Why thank you, kind sir!" I said with a smile.

"Oh. It's the mystery lady again," said the desk clerk as we entered.

"Do you have a problem with that?" demanded Philip, with a belligerence that surprised me, and turned very red.

"No--no, sir, no problem," said the desk clerk apologetically. "Just making a comment. Our motto is 'Come as you are or as the person you want to be.' Provided the basic rules are complied with, anything goes. I meant no offence."

"Oh--yeah--sorry," said Philip. Then after we'd paid our admission and parted the curtain to enter the club, he said, "I don't know what gave me the effrontery, Stella--unnecessary, I guess, but I--I feel I have to stand up for you--though I think you're perfectly capable of standing up for yourself."

"If it's is a sign of growing self-confidence, Philip, then it's a good thing," I said, smiling up at him and giving his arm a squeeze. "But you don't have to be anyone other than yourself."

"Well, I am Philip Sidney and have a name to live up to. I--I guess I'm trying to be Sir Philip Sidney, Stella's champion, her knight in shining armor."

"Philip, I'm flattered. And did you notice that he called you 'sir'? But, there. The music has just started up," I said turning to face him and placing my arms around his neck. "A lady's knight also dances with her. Would you like to?"

"Yes. I'd love to, Stella," he said, and took me into his arms and held me very close. Again I laid my head on his shoulder as we began to move to the music.

"You're wonderful, Stella," he said.

"So are you, Philip."

"No one's ever told me that before."

"It's time someone did."

--Oh Philip! I hope you'll still feel I'm wonderful when you know what I am. Oh! You say you're trying to live up to your name, Philip? Oh, how will I live up to mine! But when you know my name and who I am, surely--surely--you must want me no matter what!

Now, knowledgeable Reader, if that isn't giving it away, I don't know what is.

As we danced, a rough, scruffy looking character coming back from the bar with his drink said, as he passed by, "Hey Broad! What the hell're you hiding under that get up? Bet yer ugly as sin!"

Before I could react Philip said, "Hey! Wh--who do y--you think you're t--talking to? You--you t--t--take that back!"

"Philip," I whispered. Clearly he was putting up a brave front, but I knew he was trembling in his boots. "It's okay. No need to cause trouble."

"I--I w--w--won't let him talk about you like that, Stella," he said.

"Stella, eh?" said the tough. "Usta have an old lady named Stella. She was a real pig!"

"W--well don't you go comparing m--my Stella to yours. M--mine is no pig!"

"Talk pretty tough for a little pipsqueak," said the other, giving Philip a shove.

"Wh--who are you c--calling a--a pi--pi--pipsqueak?" demanded Philip, striving hard to be bold. "And--and wh--who do yoy think you're sh--sh--shoving? W--would you l--like to step outside and--and s--s--settle this?"

"Philip! Philip!" I protested. "You don't have to do this."

"Yes, I do, Stella," he said emphatically. "This person has insulted your honor, and I have to defend it."

"HAR! HAR! HAR!" roared the boor. "Defend her honor! What are you? Her knight in shining armor?"

"Yes. Yes, I am!" he responded, confidently. Then rather more diffidently, "W--well, maybe not in shining armor--but I am her knight!" Then once again confidently, "Now, are you going to step outside with me or not?"

"If that's what you want, Mr. Knight-in-Shining-Armor," the roughneck answered sarcastically. "Whoever y' are underneath that mask, Lady, y' better call an ambulance, because your boy friend here, your knight-in-shining-armor, is going be pounded to a pulp--a mass of blood, guts and broken bones. HAR! HAR! HAR! Come on, Mr. Hero. Let's go outside!"

"You lead the way," said Philip assertively. "I'll be right behind you!"

"Philip! Philip!" I cried, trying to hold him back. "Don't be a silly fool! You don't have to do this!"

"Yes, I do, Stella!"

"You should listen t' yer girl friend, little boy," said the roughneck. "She's got a hell of a lot more sense than you have."

"W--We'll s--see about that," said Philip.

Well, there was nothing for it. I had to follow, for I was sure Philip would need my help--that I would have to intervene with my judo and karate.

Outside in the parking lot, Philip removed his jacket and tie and handed them to me to hold.

"That's right," said his adversary. "At least save yer nice jacket and tie from getting torn to shreds the way you're gonna be. It'll be something fer yer girl friend t' remember ya by. HAR! HAR! HAR!"

Philip said nothing, but took up his stance, crouched, feet apart, fists clenched, facing his foe. I was amazed at how professional he looked. But was he really up to this? Could he really handle this thug?

"W--Well," he said, "do you mean b--b--business, or are you just going to stand there?"

"HAR! HAR! HAR!" laughed his opponent. "Been reading a book on boxing? Well, I hope yer a good reader!"

As I prepared myself to rush in to Philip's aid, his opponent reared back his fist for a blow which I feared would would shatter poor Philip's jaw and smash him to the ground. But to my surprise, Philip parried the blow and landed a hard right to his assailant's jaw, causing him to reel back, hand to his cheek, his face expressing surprise and amazement as well as pain.

"A lucky punch, but yer luck won't hold, pipsqueak," he said, lunging again at Philip who again warded off the attack and sent his opponent staggering backwards with an uppercut to the jaw. "Ow!" he cried. "Why you little--!" And again, arms flailing he charged at Philip.

Again Philip ducked the flailing arms and waded into his adversary, landing hard body blows which again sent him staggering backward. I hadn't expected this novel to take such a turn! My shy diffident lover had suddenly become a hero! And there was nothing shy and diffident about him now as he went on the offensive, landing blow after blow to his adversary's head and body until suddenly he crumpled to the ground, knocked out cold, blood streaming from his nose and mouth.

"Oh good heavens!" cried Philip. "I've killed him!"

We both stooped down beside Philip's would-be pulverizer, and I felt his neck.

"No you haven't, Philip. He's breathing and has a pulse. Some cold water will bring him around."

"I--I'll get some!" said Philip, suddenly reverting to his old, diffident self, and ran back to the Club. He soon returned with a beer glass full of water and threw it into the face of his erstwhile opponent who was already beginning to recover consciousness.

"Bl-bl-bl-bl! Help! I'm drown--W--?" cried the defeated thug, coming to and looking about him. "Wh--what happened? Who turned out the lights? Wh--what hit me?"

"My boy friend's fist" I said proudly.

"Wha--that wimp!"

"I think," I said, standing above him, hands on my hips, "he's proved he's no wimp."

"And I hope I've taught you not to insult my lady," said Philip, regaining his earlier confidence.

As the man slowly dragged himself to his feet, Philip again took up his stance, ready to hit him again if need be. His erstwhile adversary staggered, and looked around in a daze.

"Yeah, yeah. Okay, okay," he said. "For this time."

And he reeled away.

"Philip!" I cried, throwing my arms about his neck and kissing him full on the lips. "My hero! I didn't think you could do it! You told me you your boxing lessons weren't doing anything for your confidence and your heart wasn't in it, but you handled yourself magnificently--like a real professional!"

"It--it all seemed to come together, Stella, I don't know why."

"Clearly, you absorbed more than you realized," I said.

"Maybe--but I think it was something else. Um--'Having this day my horse, my hand, my lance

> Guided so well that I obtained the prize,
>
> Both by the judgment of the English eyes
>
> And of some sent from that sweet enemy France;
>
> Horsemen my skill in horsemanship advance,
>
> Townsfolk my strength; a daintier judge applies
>
> His praise to sleight which from good use doth rise;
>
> Some lucky wits impute it but to chance;
>
> Others, because of both sides I do take
>
> My blood from them who did excel in this,
>
> Think nature me a man of arms did make.
>
> How far they shot awry! The true cause is
>
> Stella looked on, and from her heav'nly face

Sent forth the beams which made so fair my race.'"

"Why Philip!" I cried. "That's from *Astrophil and Stella!* Why thank you! But--but you can't see my face."

"Your eyes and your kiss were enough!"

"Oh Philip! Oh Philip!" I said kissing him again. "It's a long time since you--I--I mean--" I stammered, with a strange fright realizing what I had been about to say, "I mean, it's a long time since I've heard that recited."

"It's along time since I--since I--" He stared at me, a look of bewilderment in his eyes. "It's a long time," he resumed, "since I first--learned it--I guess."

He put his arms around me and held me tight for some moments.

"My hero," I whispered, "you deserve your reward for your gallantry. I have a little place out in the country. Would you like to go there?"

"Oh--uh--yes! Yes, I would."

"You could even stay the night. It's Friday. You don't have to go to work in the morning."

"St--stay the night! Ohmigosh! But--but I--I don't have my pyjamas-- or my razor and tooth brush."

"We can pick up a package of razors, shaving soap, a tooth brush and tooth paste at an all night drug store--but," I said with a mischievous smile, "you won't need pyjamas."

I know this novel is set in the United States where it's "pajamas," but I had an English upbringing.

"W--well," said Philip, a bit hesitantly but soon overcoming his reservation, "okay. I--I don't mind. Uh--will you--will you--take off your mask so I can s--see your f--face when we're there?"

--Oh dear! What should I do? If I really love him--as I think I do-- and if he loves me--as I think he does--he has a right to know who I am and what I look like--there should be no secret's between us--but I'm only a character in this novel, after all, not it's author. She wants me to

62

remain Lady Enigma till the end of the novel so that the revelation of my identity will be a real surprise--though any intelligent and literate reader should have discovered who I am by now from all the hints that have been dropped; but then, what literate and intelligent person would be reading a trashy novel like this?--and is it time yet to reveal to Philip that I'm a cat burglar? Will I lose him if I do? Oh dear, oh dear! What am I to do?

What I did, was throw my arms around his neck and kiss him.

"Oh Philip!" I exclaimed. "I--I'm sorry to be so enigmatic, but--but for now--please Philip--I know it's not fair--but I--I can't explain--but Veronica wants me to remain incognito for a while longer, and it's Veronica who pulls my strings and John who pulls hers, and--Oh! It's all so complicated! So--so please bear with me for a while until--"

"A--all right, Stella," he said, disappointment, but not reproach, written all over his face and sounding in his voice. "I--I understand and I accept your right to--to remain incognito and won't press you to--to do anything Veronica doesn't want you to do because--because I--I really like you."

"Oh, Philip! You're a dear! And I like you too, Philip--very much! And I promise you, one day--"

"That's all that matters, Stella--that you will someday. I'll wait in hope."

"Oh Philip! I feel so mean presuming so on your good nature and your patience--"

"As I said before, Stella, I'm sure you have your reasons."

--And I do have reasons--but how really good are they? Good or bad, they'll have to do.

"You're really very sweet, Philip," I said aloud. "But rather than stand here talking all night in the parking lot, let's be on our way."

"Yes, let's," he said. "I--I'm looking forward to--to the rest of the evening."

"So am I Philip. I've been looking forward to it for a very long--I mean, ever since I met you."

There it was again--this sense that I--that Philip--that Philip and I--that this--this is--Oh! Can it really be that--?

"Your car's over there, Stella," said Philip interrupting my confused mental meanderings and pointing to where we had parked.

"Oh--yes. I--I'd almost forgotten where we left it."

We walked hand in hand over to the Corvette, got in and drove off. I stopped as planned at a drug store for Philip to pick up his necessities.

"Oh!" I said, spotting the business enterprise conveniently placed by Veronica next door to the drug store. "There's an all night sporting goods store. Run in and buy yourself a pair of roller-blades and knee pads."

"Roller-blades? Knee pads?" he exclaimed, his eyes starting in surprise.

"Yes. I've a long paved driveway where we can skate. I'll teach you how."

When we drove off after he made his purchases, I said, "You really surprised me tonight, Philip--very gratifyingly--by coming to my defence like that and handling that roughneck so effectively. I still can't get over it. It was so unexpected."

"I can't get over it myself, Stella," he responded, "but as I said, it was you who inspired me and gave me confidence. You made me feel like my great namesake--almost as though I really were Sir Philip Sidney."

"Oh Philip!" I exclaimed. "I think almost that you are--I mean--I mean--"

"That it was as though his spirit had entered me and gave me the courage and the strength?"

"Yes--something like that."

"I sort of felt that too. Strange, isn't it."

"It--it is strange, Philip--very strange," I said as we passed the outskirts of East Clintwood and I pressed down on the gas pedal and, hoping there were no highway patrolmen around, sent the Corvette speeding down the open road. "Anyway, I'm very proud of you."

"Thank you. Stella. It makes me feel nine feet tall to hear you say that--and--well--if I do say so myself--I feel rather proud of myself too."

"And why shouldn't you, Philip?"

"I don't know, I was always told that one should always be modest about one's accomplishments and not brag."

"Well, I suppose there's some truth in that--I hate a blow-hard--but I don't see why one shouldn't take some pride in one's achievements."

"If bashing someone about is an achievement. I hate violence, really."

"Yes, I see what you mean, but you were not the aggressor, Philip."

"No, I suppose not. I had to defend your honor."

--My honor! What honor has a cat burglar? A perverted one, I suppose. Well, I do have my honor as a woman, and that's what he meant, I'm sure. How trusting he is!

Just at that moment we arrived at the entrance to my secluded little cottage on a backwater of the Clintwood River near the Clint Wood, and so I was saved from any further conscience cudgeling.

"Here's my place," I said, and I turned the Corvette into the tree-lined driveway. "Too bad it's night time. You can't see what a lovely spot it is--and we're too late for the sunset which is usually quite glorious. But there'll be another time."

"I'll see the view in the morning."

"Why don't you just stay for the weekend, Philip?"

"Oh--uh--I--I've a ticket for the Symphony on Saturday night. B--but I sh--shouldn't p--put the Symphony before you."

"Oh no, Philip. You must go," I said as I brought the Corvette to a stop in front of my cottage. "I would, if I were in your place. What is being played?"

"Mahler's Tenth Symphony in the revised Derycke Cooke performing version--one doesn't get many opportunities to hear it."

"No, indeed. You must go Philip. I won't feel hurt."

--Actually, I'd almost forgotten that I had a ticket for the concert too. That should prove interesting! I'll let him see me without my mask but not tell him who I am! Oh dear! Aren't I awful!

As we got out of the car, Philip looked up at the sky.

"Oh my gosh!" he exclaimed. "The stars! Myriads of them! They're so overwhelming! We city dwellers never see them like this!"

"That's one of the reasons I like to come out here, Philip. I'm an urban person at heart, but I like to get away sometimes to experience nature in all its vastness and mystery."

"The brightest stars are in your eyes Stella,"

"Oh Philip! You say the nicest things!"

Just then, from inside my dog barked.

"You have a dog out here? Who looks after him when you're not here?"

"Actually, she's a her. I brought her out here earlier today because--because I was planning to spend the weekend here anyway. She enjoys it out here."

"I'm sure she must. What kind is she?"

"The best kind--a mutt."

"They are the best--healthy, good natured--no problems arising from overbreeding."

"You know dogs, I see."

"We always had a dog at home--and always a mutt. What do you call her?"

"Astarte."

"Astarte! The moon goddess?"

"Yes, I guess that's right. Actually, I named her after the beloved woman in Byron's *Manfred*. But let's go in so you can meet her."

We walked up the few steps to the porch, and when I unlocked and opened the door and flicked on a light, Astarte, my white Lab-St. Bernard cross, with reddish brown ears and face mask and three large reddish brown spots on her back, came bounding toward us barking. Philip went down on one knee, held out the back of his hand toward her so she could sniff him, and spoke in quiet, friendly tones to her.

"Hello, Astarte. I'm a friend of your mistress."

"Yes, Astarte," I said kneeling down and placing an arm around Philip's shoulder. "Philip is all right. He's a friend."

Within seconds, Astarte was letting him stroke and pat her.

"You're a very nice girl, Astarte," he said.

"Well," I said, "I can see you two are going to get on very well. Come on in Philip," I said, rising.

Astarte, wagging her tail and making a great fuss over Philip, followed us in. If I needed any further confirmation that Philip was the right man, I had it in Astarte's quick acceptance of him.

"This is a very comfortable looking place, Stella," he said as he gazed about him. "You've fixed it up very nicely."

"Actually, my father built it, and my mother did most of the furnishing--though I've added a few touches since it has been mine."

"Your parents are both dead?"

"Yes--in an accident."

"I'm sorry, Stella."

"Thank you. It was a few years ago, and it's behind me--mostly. There are times when I really miss them."

"I'm sure you do. Was your father a carpenter by trade, Stella--or a builder?" he asked as he examined the log walls. "It appears to be very well constructed."

"No. It was just a hobby--one he really enjoyed and was good at. He was--he was a--a locksmith."

"Oh?" he said, turning back to me. "Interesting."

--If only you knew, Philip! Oh dear! The skeleton in my closet! It's not that he was a bad man--really--but--but--Oh dear! Oh dear! I've so much to confess and to try to explain! But not right now. Not until--

"Oh!" said Philip spotting the instrument hung on the wall! "A guitar! Do you play it?"

"A little."

"I bet you're very good."

"I--I don't get much time to play it lately. Do you play?"

"Yes--a little--well, quite a bit actually."

"Then play it, Philip. I'd love to hear you."

"Oh--well--gee--I'm not an Andres Segovia or a Narciso Yepes."

"That's not the same as saying you don't play well. Here," I said taking down the guitar and handing it to him. "Will you something for me, Philip?"

"For you--for Stella? All right. I'd love to play--for you. I hope my playing is worthy of you."

And he played Morena Toroba's "Recuerdos a la Alhambra" with it's haunting melody over a tremolo bass.

"Philip!" I exclaimed when he had finished! "That was wonderful! You're a very accomplished player!"

"I've lot's of time to practice. I'm alone a lot."

"Not any more, Philip," I said putting my arms around him.

"No--not any more--not as much--not nearly as much--thanks to you, Stella."

"And you never need to be again, Philip. But--but I should change."

"Change?"

"Into something a little more--um--comfortable."

"Oh--"

"I won't be long," I said, releasing him from my embrace and heading toward the stairs to my bedroom. "Play something else while I'm gone."

"All right. This is by Dowland."

"You know, Philip," I called back, "with your ability to come to your lady's defence and your ability to serenade her on your lute--I mean your guitar--and to recite poetry, you're a real Renaissance man--as Ophelia said of Hamlet, the scholar, soldier, courtier."

"I--I'm not soldier or courtier, but still, I do sometimes feel like a Renaissance man--almost that I--but that's silly."

"Almost what?" I said, turning back to him. "Tell me."

"You'll laugh."

"No, I won't laugh, Philip."

"I'm sure it's just because I've read so much about it and enjoy its literature and music, but it's almost as though--as though I--I was there. Now that is silly, isn't it?"

--No Philip, it isn't silly. No it's not silly at all. I think it's--"

"You're not laughing," he said.

"No, Philip," I said, bemused. "I'm not."

"I guess people get feelings like that some times."

"Yes, Philip, I'm sure they do. But--but play the Dowland piece for me."

"It's a Pavane."

"Oh! I used to love to da--I'd love to hear a Pavane again. Uh--M--my father used to play them."

He started to play, and I ran up the stairs to my bedroom.

--Oh! I said to myself, clutching myself and leaning against the wall to steady myself, for I felt light-headed and giddy, almost as Hamlet felt after meeting his father's ghost. I had to sit on the bed for a few minutes before I could recover my composure. It's true! I said to myself. It's true!

Once I was in control of myself again, I removed the corsage Philip had bought me--Gee, he's thoughtful!--and slipped out of my cat suit and cowl and into a body stocking of a kind of simulated black lace, pinned my corsage

69

to it, put on my red half mask and red high heels and donned an auburn fall made from my own once long hair which I'd had cut short and shaped to my head when I took up cat burgling so that my cowl would fit more easily. I paused a moment before I returned, somewhat apprehensively, to the living area, for it was a shame to interrupt such lovely playing and because I feared he might think my attire too sleazy or kinky--which it was, but this is that kind of novel, after all--but I wasn't sure he was ready to see me completely naked. Absorbed as he was in his playing, he did not at first notice me. When he did look up, he stopped playing in the middle of a passage and stared open mouthed at me as I descended the stairs.

To my great gratification, he exclaimed, "Stella! You--you're beautiful!"

"You--you don't think my get-up is too sleazy or kinky?"

"I think you--you're very--a--a--alluring!"

He rose, set aside the guitar and came to me.

"I'm sorry to interrupt your beautiful playing," I said as we embraced.

"I--I'd rather do this," he replied and lifted me into his arms.

--Oh Philip! You get better and better!

And he was great when he took me to my bed. All his inhibitions completely overcome, he gently stripped me of my body stocking and high heels--in the reverse order, actually. And then--Oh Philip! I'm sure your namesake could not have been a better lover! But Stella never knew, for when

> In a grove most rich of shade,
> Where birds wanton musicke made,
> May then yong his pide weedes showing,
> New perfumed with flowers fresh growing,
> Astrophel with Stella sweete,
> Did for mutual comfort meete...

...she spake; her speech was such,

As not eares but hart did tuch:...

Astrophel sayd she, my love

Cease in these effects to prove:

Now be still, yet still believe me,

Thy grief more then death doth greave me.

If that any thought in me,

Can taste comfort but of thee,

Let me fed with hellish anguish,

Joyless, hopelesse, endlesse languish.

If those eyes you praised, be

Halfe so deere as you to me,

Let me home returne stark blinded

Of these eyes, and blunder minded....

Therefore, Deere, this no more move,

Least though I leave not thy love,

Which too deep in me is framed,

I should blush when thou art named.

Therewithall away she went,

Leaving him so passion rent,

With what she had done and spoken,

That therewith my song is broken.


But oh what great joy! This time I did not leave my love. But oh! Will he love me when he knows what I am?

# Chapter Seven

We spent the following day swimming in my pool--it was sunny and my body suit dries quickly--and rollerblading on the driveway. Though Philip had never rollerbladed, and I had to lead him through the first steps, he soon gained confidence--he just needs a bit of encouragement to be a more assertive person--and became quite proficient. Then, in the evening I drove him back to his apartment.

I had barely time to get back to my town house to change to go to the concert hall and take my seat at the auditorium for the symphony. Poor Philip! I felt really badly that he had to sit up in the back row of the balcony while I had a choice seat in the orchestra. I wore my green gown with gold shoes and my blond wig--which surprised the people who occupy the neighboring seats to mine--for I didn't want Philip to identify me by my auburn hair. Oh dear! This masquerade of mine really is silly, but, as I said, Veronica wants it that way. I looked about to try to find Philip, and at last I saw him in the gallery.

With the main work so long, the first part of the program consisted simply of an overture--Beethoven's Second Leonore Overture. At intermission, then, I sought out Philip in the rotunda and arranged to bump into him--I mean really bump into him--in the line for coffee.

"Oh! *Je vous demande pardon, M'sieur,*" I said adopting my French maid's accent. "I am verree sorree."

"Oh--*Il n'y a pas de quoi, Mademoiselle.*"

"*J'ai peur*--I am afraid zat I am verree clumsee."

"Not at all. There is quite a crush, and it's easy to be jostled."

"You are verree undairstandeeng, *M'sieur.* I was going to obtain *une tasse de café*--a cup of coffee. Per'aps by way of apologee I could buy one for *M'sieur* also?"

"Oh--*Merci, Mademoiselle,* but that's hardly necessary."

"*M'sieur rougis*--eet eez zat you blush, *M'sieur.* Per'aps eet eez that *M'sieur 'as une petite amie--comment vous dites?*--'ow you say?--a girl friend?--and so 'e feel zat 'e would be deesloyal?"

"I do have a girl friend, yes. I don't think she's the jealous type and would mind, but still--"

--Oh Philip! Your loyalty makes me very happy!

"I undairstand, *M'sieur.* I do not weesh to--'ow you say?--jeopardize *M'sieur's* relationsheep weeth 'ees young ladee. She eez preettee, *votre petite amie*--your girl friend?"

"Uh--yes, she is."

"You 'esitate, *M'sieur.* She eez not preettee? Eet eez not ze most eemportant sing, *M'sieur,* zat she should be preettee."

"Oh, she's pretty, all right. Hers is a beauty that--that grows on one."

--Oh Philip! I love you! I'm being awfully mean, I know. I shouldn't be playing games with you or testing your loyalty like this, for I don't really believe it needs to be tested, but you are standing up wonderfully! But oh! Will your loyalty stand up when the real test comes? If it does not, I can hardly blame you. I just hope that it will and that who I am will matter to you more than what I am.

"She has lovely eyes," said Philip interrupting my reverie, "rather," he added hesitantly, "like yours--and beautiful, full lips--also rather like yours--" For some moments he stared at me, furrowing his brow--"but she has auburn hair--lovely auburn hair."

"Hauburn 'air! Zat does eendeed sound lovelee, M'sieur. I 'ave often weeshed zat my 'air were hauburn. *Votre petite amie*--your girl friend eendeed sounds very attracteeve."

"I'm a very lucky man."

--Oh, thank you Philip! I hope you'll always think so! It's I who am lucky!

"I sink zat per'aps she eez also a veree luckee young woman."

"I--I hope she thinks so--because she's a very remarkable person."

--Oh Philip! I love you more each time you speak!

"But your girl friend, she eez not 'ere weez you tonight, M'sieur?"

"Uh--no. I--uh--bought my ticket long before I met her--and the concert was sold out."

"Ah! *Cela, c'est tres triste,* M'sieur. Zat eez veree sad."

"I'm sure we'll manage to be here together some day."

--Oh Philip! I hope so!

"But there's the bell calling us back to our seats. It's been nice talking to you--but I'm afraid you never got your cup of coffee."

"*Il n'y a pas de quoi, M'sieur.* Eet 'as been a pleasure to talk weez you also. I weesh you 'appiness weez your *petite amie.*"

"I call her Stella, but that's not her real name."

"Oh? Vraiment? *Stella--Étoile*--Star. Eez zat not w'at Pheeleep Seedney called 'ees lovair?"

"Uh--yes--yes it is. Hm."

Again he gave me a curious, penetrating stare.

"W'at eez eet, M'sieur? You seem--'ow you say--perplexed?"

"Oh--no--nothing. Just thought of a strange coincidence."

Was he tumbling to the truth? But before we could converse any longer, a voice came over the intercom urging us to return to our seats.

"*Bon soir, M'am'selle,*" he said. "I hope you enjoy the rest of the concert."

"*Merci, M'sieur,*" I replied. "*Et vous, aussi. Bon soir.*"

My heart all aflutter, I returned to my seat. I'm not sure if I even heard the rest of the concert--but from that moment I would always think of Mahler's Tenth Symphony in the Revised Derycke Cooke Performing Version as our song.

# CHAPTER EIGHT

Matter's are coming to a head! I must wind up my operations as a cat burglar. But I still want the painting, the rubies and the emeralds. I could, of course, buy the jewels--I'm perfectly able to--but it's much more fun to steal them. I mean, as I said, I like the adventure--and it's in my blood.

A week ago last Monday I had been at the Penthouse in my role as Madeleine de la Fontaine, French maid of impeccable qualifications and character. As I dusted in the living room, I stopped to contemplate the painting, the *Troisieme Étude* of Charles Camille Duparc, one of France's greatest living abstract artists, where it hung upside down above the mantel of the fire place.

"Ah, Madeleine!" said my employer, suddenly and unexpectedly entering the room. "I see you looking at that painting. What do you think of it? I don't know what to make of it, really. My husband bought it--paid an absolutely exorbitant price for it, in my opinion, but he says it's by one of Europe's leading artists and that owning such a painting gives us real distinction, shows we have taste and refinement. But really, I don't know. I'm very perplexed by it. What is it meant to be? Perhaps as a French woman, you have some understanding of such things."

I felt like telling her it was meant simply to be a painting, as a Mozart symphony is meant only to be a Mozart symphony, to be enjoyed simply for itself, for as Picasso said, "People who try to explain pictures are usually barking up the wrong tree." But in my role as an employee I must not say that sort of thing. Also I had to be careful. If I showed too much understanding and appreciation, it would throw suspicion my way when suddenly the painting went missing--as I fully intended it should.

"Not everee one een France eez arteesteec, Madame. I am onlee a seemple girl from ze suburbs of Paree, not a connoisseur of ze art."

"Well, do you like it, Madeleine?"

"Forgeeve me for sayeeng so, Madame, but I do not really know. But zen, as I say, Madame, I know so veree leetle about ze art."

"I don't either, Madeleine, but I have to confess, I don't like it. I wish it was not hanging on my wall."

Though she should, of course, have used the subjunctive--"were" rather than "was"--I fully intended that her wish would soon be granted.

"Per'aps, Madame," I said, acting on a whim, "eet would look bettair hupside down." Whereupon I turned around, bent over--fortunately I had the dark wig I always wear as Madeleine de la Fontaine well fastened on; it would have blown my cover if it had flopped onto the floor at my feet--and, grasping my knees from behind, looked at the picture from between my shapely legs--as the heroine, of course, my legs could hardly be anything other than shapely, their shapeliness beautifully enhanced, of course, by my high heels and shown to perfection by my very short skirt.

"Oh dear! I could never do that!" gasped my employer.

"Per'aps eef Madame were to attend some feetness classes--bot ze painteeng does look bettair from zis angle."

"Surely Jacques Bouchard and Lucien Parizeau Framers Inc. didn't frame it upside down! They are supposed to be the best in East Clintwood. What will my husband think!"

--They have probably framed it right side up, I said to myself, but you, Madame, have certainly hung it upside down.

Just as I straightened up again, I heard a long, low whistle and turned to see its perpetrator, a young man, entering the room.

"Well! Who have we here!" he exclaimed.

He should, of course, have said "whom."

"Oh!" said my employer. "John! I didn't hear you come in. Madeleine, this is my son John home from a holiday in Las Vegas, Hollywood and Disney Land. John, this is Madeleine de la Fontaine, my cleaning lady--uh--that is, I mean, the French maid I employ on a once-a-week basis."

"Enchanty, Madamwawzel!" he said in an abominable imitation of French, grasping my hand to kiss it and bowing affectedly. He looked momentarily rather crestfallen as I quickly and unceremoniously withdrew my hand but then continued on in his breezy, pseudo-urbane manner, "The Mater mentioned that she had hired you in one of her letters, but she didn't say that you were so gorgeous."

Such witless misplacing of his modifier! Hired me in one her letters! Like the elephant in Groucho Marx's pyjamas or the man with a wooden leg named Bill!

"'Ow do you do, *M'sieur*," I said coolly.

"I don't know why you were bent over like that, Madamwawzel," John went on, "but the posture sure showed off your gorgeous legs!"

"Now John! Really!" protested his mother.

"Well, Mater, she does have gorgeous legs--and everything else is pretty gorgeous too. You will forgive me, Madamwawzel," he said, "but I cannot help expressing my appreciation of such great pulchritude when I encounter it."

Much better Philip's shyness than this nouveau riche clod's brassiness and pretension!

"You flatter me, M'sieur," I said, *avec sang froid*. (In this episode I am meant, after all, to be French.)

"We were just talking about the painting your father spent so much money on, John," said his mother. "Madeleine wondered if it might look better upside down. That's why she was bent over."

"You know, Mater," he said, "I really can't understand why the Pater purchased it, except, of course, as an investment. Perhaps Madamwawzel is right. Maybe it does look better upside down."

Whereupon he turned around and bent down to look at it between his legs. (Whether or not they were shapely--in a strong, muscular, masculine way, of course--I could not tell because he was wearing trousers. All I know is that I had to resist very strenuously the desire forcibly to project the pointy toe of my right high heeled shoe into his buttocks. Kick him in the pants, in other words.)

"Can't say I see much difference," he said, standing up, red faced and panting. (He could lose a little girth around the middle.)

Then he turned again to look at me with a decided anticipation of the bedroom and proceeded to undress me with his eyes.

"But to get back to our more interesting first topic, how is it, Madamwawzel dee lah Fountain--uh, I hope I may call you Madeleine--and please call me John..."

"Zat eez being too--'ow you say?--fameeliair too soon, M'sieur--even eef I am onlee, as your mozair says, ze cleaneeng ladee."

"Oh--uh--perhaps in your country, Mademoiselle, but here in America we don't waste time on formalities."

"Eet eez deefeecult to break weeth one's upbreengeeng and tradeetions, M'sieur."

"I understand, Madeleine--Madamwawzel--but I hope you will try," he said, fluttering his eye lids more rapidly than a humming bird its wings.

"Een time, per'aps. M'sieur."

Oh yes! Much better Philip's shy decency!

"But I'm puzzled. How is it that a gorgeous young woman like you has to make her living as a cleaning lady--as a maid?"

Quick, Veronica! Come up with a plausible explanation. Ah! Here it is! Thank you.

"I came over 'ere oreegeenallee as an *au pair* girl workeeng for a weedow 'oo died suddainlee before I 'ad earned enough monee to return to France. So I 'ave 'ired myself out as a maid. Aftair all, a girl 'as to make a leeveeng some'ow--as *Mademoiselle* Veronique Veritee says een ze Preface to one of 'er ozair novels."

"Oh--sorry to hear that--but surely you could have done other things. With your looks, you could have been a model--"

Now, why did I not become a model? Think, Veronica! Quick! (Sorry to put so much pressure on you, Veronica. I know, from the way you've kept deleting and changing speeches and moving passages up and down your computer screen, that you've been having difficulties with this episode. I hope, though, that you get it right soon. It has all been making me rather dizzy.)

"I am too shy, M'sieur."

"You shouldn't be. But it is very strange you came here as an oh pear girl. Doesn't that 'dee lah' in your name indicate aristocracy?"

"Oh?" queried his mother in surprise. "Madeleine? Is that true? You never said anything of this!"

In stories like this, the protagonist at this point in the narrative always has some sort of foreshadowing, some sort of augury, some foretelling that to act in an unusual way will be advantageous, and that is what happened now. Something told me I should go along with John's supposition, and so I replied, "I deed not theenk eet eemportant, *Madame*, but w'at your son says eez true. Ze possesseeve 'de' weeth ze arteecle 'la' does eendeecate nobeeleetee, but *helas, Madame*, ze fameelee fell on veree bad times aftair ze Revolution, and *dans une republique* nobeeleetee counts for veree leetle

80

unless one 'as retained one's wealth. Furzairmore, ze true line of *les Comtes de la Fontaine* 'as died out a long time ago. I am of a veree eenferior line--a cadet line, as zey say."

One of the great advantages of being in a novel rather than in real life is that it's always convenient to be able to fall back on the kind of improbabilities that have helped many a protagonist out of a jam, for I had investigated the la Fontaine line--serendipitously while looking up something else--and found that though there may be surviving members of the family, they have not yet been traced. When I came to choose a name for myself as a French maid, de la Fontaine just automatically popped into my head, as they say--whoever "they" are.

"Ah! but still," said John, "you are nobility!"

"Oh dear!" exclaimed his mother. "I should probably be calling you 'Your majesty'!"

How easily some people are impressed!

"I seenk ze appropriate address eez 'Your Grace'--or een France, *Mademoiselle la Comtesse*--but we do not know yet zat I am *une comtesse*. At ze moment, I am seemplee *Mademoiselle de la Fontaine*. You may be makeeng too much of ze areestocrateek form *de mon nom*."

"Perhaps, then, Madamwawzel--if you don't feel it's beneath you--"

Oh dear! What was coming next?--as if I didn't know!

"Een my present circumstances, M'sieur, zere eez leetle zat eez beneath me. I am, aftair all, just ze 'umble workeeng girl. "

"Oh but a very attractive one and one with and aristocratic background."

"But a long time ago, M'sieur."

"But you have it nevertheless, and so, if you're agreeable, I would be real proud if you would accept my invitation to attend Susan van Alstyne's farewell recital--not that I'm all that fond of classical music, but we have to keep up appearances."

"Oh!" exclaimed my employer. "Please do come with us, Madeleine--uh--Your Grace--uh Countess. We would be so-o-o much obliged!"

"But--but--*Madame, M'sieur*--I do not really belong weeth soch deesteengueeshed companee as your friends."

"What!" said John. "With the blood of royalty flowing in your veins!"

"'Ardlee royaltee. M'sieur, but zough, for w'at eet eez worth, and zat eez, I am afraid not veree much now, I may be ze last repreesentateeve of a noble 'ouse, ze noble blood eez veree much deelutedby ze blood of *le bourgeoisie et les sans culottes--le peuple--le tiers état.*"

They ignored my deliberately assumed snobbery. But then, they probably could not understand the French. How easy it is for people to believe what they want to believe. Though very tangled webs we weave when first we practice to deceive, I was enjoying having such great fun at their expense. Oh! I really am a nasty little girl!

"Well, never mind all that. All that really matters is that you're gorgeous," retorted John. "In America, that makes you royalty. What do you say, Madeleine--Madamwawzel? Will you be my date?"

Philip had gone out of town for a few days for an aunt's funeral, so I would not be seeing him for a while. (He'd left me a most apologetic note on his apartment door for me to pick up one night when I was to call for him and take him to the Gemini Club. What else could he do when he didn't know any other way to reach me?) I wondered if I were to accept this invitation, would it be a betrayal of him. But something told me that if I did accept, a golden opportunity would open to me.

--Oh Philip! Philip! Please forgive me for playing this game with you! I promise you, I won't really betray you, for I know what he wants, but I've never had any problem dealing with that sort of thing!

"I am told," I said to them, "zat *Mademoiselle* van Alstyne eez a veree fine seengair. I would veree much like to 'ear 'er."

"Though why it is she has that Imogen Edwards girl from the other side of the tracks as her accompanist, I don't know," said my employer. "They say, in fact, that she's Manfred Andreotti the Crime Boss's mistress. But you will be our guest--John's guest--*Mademoiselle la Comtesse?*"

"*Oui*--yes. I weell go weeth you eef zat eez w'at you weesh."

"Gee!" cried John. "Gee! This is wonderful--a date with a real gorgeous woman and a countess to boot! Wow!"

Suddenly, the prospect of an association with French nobility appeared very propitious for them. It would give the family class--so they thought.

"Zere may be," I said, "zose zere 'oo weell recognize me as zeir French maid and cleaneeng ladee."

"Then we will just have to disabuse them and introduce you as a countess."

"I weell wear my auburn weeg, M'sieur, and per'aps I weell not be recognized."

"Oh--well--all right. Actually, I like auburn. It will go especially well with your blue eyes. Strange. Blue eyes, dark hair."

"Zat eez ze result, *comme j'ai dit*, of ze meexture of proletarian, peasant, bourgeois and also some Breton blood een my veins, M'sieur."

"But the aristocratic blood is still there!"

"*Eh bien*, a leetle--*peut etre un peu de gouttes*--a few drops," I said.

"I bet a whole lot of drops!"

Boy! Once some people latch on to something that seems to give them distinction, even by association, they won't give it up! Strange how we Americans with all our vaunted democratic and republican egalitarianism are still awed by royalty and aristocracy.

"One should dress formallee, M'sieur, for ze recital?" I asked.

"Yes. But don't worry if you don't have a dress! We'll take you out and get something right now!"--Yes, and what you put on me you'll assume the right to take off me!

"I 'ave a green brocade eveneeng gown zat weell be quite appropriate, I seenk. Eet was a geeft."

"Oh!" cried my employer. "An emerald necklace and ear rings would look marvelous with such a dress! Or would rubies be better--a nice contrast? But I imagine the Vanderhafen twins will be there, otherwise, I'd try to borrow--well, now John, is it Yolande who wears the emeralds and Beatrix the rubies, or the other way around?"

"I think, Mater," said John, "that they interchange them to confuse people. Just as soon as everyone thinks it's Yolande who wears the emeralds and Beatrix the rubies, they interchange them and make everyone flustered when they address them by the wrong names."

"Eet eez all right," I said. "I 'ave some appropriate jewelry--geefts from my dear *Maman et Papa* before zey died."

In fact, I do have some appropriate jewelry, and it *was* the gift of my mother and father, so I won't be in danger of being caught wearing the jewelry stolen from some of those I might meet at the recital. But oh! Emeralds! Rubies! What I've been wanting for so long! The Vanderhafen twins are a pair of precious little snobs, so I won't mind stealing their jewels--not that I've ever really minded stealing anyone's jewels. But as I said in the first chapter, I do it for the fun and adventure rather than for what I gain from it--well, more or less for the fun than for the gain. I do, as I said, keep a few things for myself--and I will keep the rubies and emeralds! I knew there was a reason for my going along with all this flim-flam about my being a countess! Everything is falling into place. I fear now, though, I can't steal the painting outright, but Glen Campbell and Gordon Clark, the forgers, fabricators and fakers, could make a copy of it from a print in an art book so that I could sneak in some night and make a substitution and no one would be the wiser. But I think I must go for the Vanderhafen jewels the same night as the recital. Oh Philip! Soon I will have achieved all my goals and be able to give up all this and tell you who I really am, and I hope--oh how I hope!--you won't reject me when you know the truth--for we must be together at last! We must!

"Well, then," began John--if you, reader, can remember what was going on before that long digression, he and I were making a date to go to a recital--"can I pick you up at about--?"

--Oh, no! I mustn't be called for at home!

"Ah, M'sieur!" I said. "I 'ave to work late zat eveneeng. Eet eez bettair zat I come 'ere. I weell take my gown to work and change zere."

"Oh, gee, that's rather awkward. Couldn't--?"

"Eet eez no trouble, M'sieur."

Well, the night of the recital came, and must say I looked quite stunning in my green dress, silver shoes and silver jewelry--and auburn hair--but not as stunning a Miss Imogen Edwards, Miss Van Alstyne's accompanist. She is gorgeous! I mean, I am the heroine and I am attractive, and I've always thought I had nice breasts--and I do--but hers! What I wouldn't give--! And that long, flowing hair! Mine is nice enough, but even when I let it grow long, it just falls straight; it doesn't flow! I know women's liberation says we are not to concern ourselves about such matters, but as a pianist I once met said about the Labecque sisters, even though the important thing is that they are brilliant pianists and sensitive artists, their being beautiful women does them no harm. So, yes, I am more than a little bit jealous of Imogen Edwards. And she plays the piano to boot!

However, when after the recital I was introduced to the Vanderhafen twins--wearing, I noted without drawing undue attention to my doing so, their emeralds and rubies--as *Mademoiselle la Comtesse de la Fontaine*, I was gratified, stuck up young twits though they are, that they were quite overcome on being introduced to a countess--to me, that is.

"Oh my! A Countess! A real countess!" cried Twin One.

"Oh! How lovely!" exclaimed Twin Two. "Such rare refinement!"

"Delightful!" said the first. "Such elegance!"

"Will you be staying in East Clintwood long, Countess?" asked the other. "We'd love to get to know you. Do say you'll be here a while. Perhaps we could meet for a cocktail."

"I am afraid, *Mesdemoiselles*, zat I am leaveeng for France wizzin a day or two and I weell be veree busee."

John looked at me in some surprise, opened his mouth as though to speak, but I kicked him sereptitiously on the ankle, and he said nothing.

"Oh!" exclaimed Twin One. "How devastating--I mean I'm sorry."

"Why is it," asked Twin Two, "that we did not read about your visit in the social columns?"

"I like to remain eencogneeto, *M'am'selle*," I said. "I like to avoid ze publeeceetee."

"Oh," said Twin One. "That's very strange."

"Publeeceetee can be veree tryeeng," I said.

"I never found it so," said Twin Two, "but then, unfortunately, I'm not a countess." Clearly they were girls who liked the limelight. "But it has been very nice meeting you. Perhaps if you're in East Clintwood again--"

"Yes," said Twin One reaching into her handbag. "Here is our card. Please look us up."

"Eef evair I come back, *Mesdemoiselles. Mais alors*, eet 'as geeven me great pleasure to meet such charmeeng young ladees."

--Oh, you'll never know how much pleasure!

"It has been wonderful meeting you, Countess," began Twin Two, "and I do hope we can meet again. Perhaps when we visit France--"

"I am afraid zat I move around quite a beet all ovair ze Conteenent. I cannot geeve any kind of assurance zat I weell be 'ome w'en you come. Een fact, I 'ave no permanent reseedence. I make my 'ome een 'otel rooms or weeth friends. As I was telleeng M'sieur Jean, my fameelee's eenhereetance was confeescated at ze time of ze Revolution. All I' ave left eez *mon titre--*my title--wheech *dans une republique* eez a veree emptee sing of leetle conseequence."

"Oh, but it does mean something--certainly to us," said Twin One. "And please, as my sister said--as I think she meant to say--please keep in touch."

"I weell try."

--I'll be in touch sooner than you want me to be!

The sisters made their good-byes, and very soon afterwards, having an intuition that I had to act tonight if I were to obtain the jewels, I pleaded tiredness after a long day, and making profuse apologies, I begged John that we might leave. He was most accommodating, no doubt from anticipation of a pleasure which I felt no qualms about denying him, and took me back to their apartment building where I had left my car--around a corner and on a back street facing away from the building so that he would not see it when I drove away.

"What was that about leaving for France in a few days, Madeleine--uh--Madamwawzelle la Countess?" he asked.

"Eet was seemply--'ow you say?--a ploy--a decepceeon to keep zem from tryeeng to look me hup. I do not weesh to be eenvolved weeth zem socialee. I am not reallee in zeir sphere."

"Yeah, I sort of thought it might be something like that, but, geez! as a countess--"

"As I said I am not reallee a countess--hat least I am not so recognized by ze French government."

"Heck! Nobody knows that over here. But perhaps you would like to come up for a night cap?" he said, looking at me with bedroom eyes.

"A night cap, M'sieur? My 'ead does not get cold w'en I am sleepeeng. Eef eet deed, I would get one myself."

"Oh--uh--sorry. It's American slang. Means a drink--a cocktail or something."

"Oh, no sank you, M'sieur. I' ave 'ad enough to dreenk zis eveneeng. Eet 'as been a great pleasure, zough. Sank you veree much for takeeng me. I enjoyed ze recital. Mademoiselle Van Alstyne, she 'as a lovelee voice, *n'est ce pas?*"

"Uh--yeah she has. Uh--look--I was hoping--"

"Zat you might see me again? I must zink about zat, M'sieur. Eet 'as all been so veree sudden. I weell--'ow you say?--let you know."

"Oh--well--gee--I--"

*"Ainsi, M'sieur, bon soir,"* I said, opening the car door to get out. "I 'ave enjoyed ze eveneeng. *Merci bien, et bon soir*--sank you and good-night."

"Oh--well at least let me drive you to your car."

"Eet eez all right, M'sieur. Eet eez not far, and I weell enjoy ze walk."

"Well, may I at least kiss you good night?" he asked, leaning toward me as I started to slip out the door.

"Oh, M'sieur. You are being--'ow you say?--too advanced? *Non, non.* Too progressive? *Non, non.* Ah! *Oui!* Too forward."

"But I thought French girls--"

"'Ave loose morals, M'sieur, and do not care w'at zey do? Zat eez a gross deescourteesee and eensult to French woman'ood! Besides, I am of ze areestocracee and you, M'sieur, are but a commonair!"

My turn to be a snob!

"Wh--!"

"I 'ave decided, M'sieur seence you 'ave raised ze mattair, to look eento ze posseebeeleetee of claimeeng mon titre. Bonsoir, M'sieur. Good night," I said and got out of the car.

"Damn!" I heard him as I walked away.

--Whew! What I have to go through some times! Now, to drive away some place where I could change to Lady Enigma before proceeding to the Vanderhafen residence. And I think, Veronica, this is probably a good place to start a new chapter. After all, you have to figure out how I'm going to pull off this next stunt.

# Chapter Nine
## (That many! Already!)

The Vanderhafen residence was a very large and sumptuous mansion with a long, tree-lined driveway leading up to the front. I had driven past it several times in the days and evenings preceding the day before Van Alstyne recital and had obtained some sense of the lay out, and I had also checked a reliable authority on the security system; but as I've said before, you'll have to wait till the end of the novel to learn the identity of that reliable authority. Now, after I had parked on a side street and walked in my sexy, all-conceiling head-to-toe form-fitting black costume, to the iron fence surrounding the house and lurked in some shrubbery to await the Vanderhafen's arrival. I had not lurked long before the Vanderhafen limousine pulled into the driveway. Taking advantage of the temporary opening in the security system--by the luck of heroines of trashy novels, I was right on time--I slipped into the yard and hid behind a tree--a great maple--until the gate closed. Then with my handy little device I deactivated the security system for my getaway--naturally I could not do that before hand, for that would have made them suspicious--and, crouching low, I ran toward the house, staying well within the shadow of the trees. I hid behind another great maple and watched as the chauffeur opened the limousine door for the twins and their parents to get out and mount the front steps to enter the house. Once they were inside and the chauffeur had driven the limo to the garage, I moved quickly but stealthily in the shadow of the terrace and up the steps and hid myself among some patio furniture. The rest would be easy. It was just a matter now of waiting until the house was dark and quiet. I hoped it would not be long.

After about a quarter of an hour, the living room lights went out and I moved to the door. With my handy little gadget, I was able to deactivate the security system, and then it was a simple matter to pick the lock. Oh, I'm a very skilled burglar. I had a very good teacher, as you shall hear. I entered the hallway where only a little blue night light glowed, looked about--one should always do that in this line of work (not that I'm recommending that anyone take it up)--listened--one should also always do that--and quietly relocked the door in case anyone came to check--which someone did almost right away. I had just time to hide among some coats and cloaks in the alcove provided for such items when one of the servants came into the hallway and walked to the door and tried the handle. Satisfied that all was well--oh, if only he had known!--he returned the way he came. I withdrew from my hiding place and proceeded to the stairs. A light still shone from the upstairs hallway, and so I climbed cautiously only as far as the landing where again I crouched in the shadows. From an open bedroom door I heard the twins talking to each other.

"Do you suppose that woman really is a French countess?" asked Twin One.

"Why do you ask? Why shouldn't she be?" responded Twin Two. "She looked like a countess. I mean look at the way she dressed."

"Yes, I suppose--though any rich woman could dress like that."

"That's true enough, but she had the manners--the style--the air. What makes you think she wasn't?"

"I don't know. Perhaps it's just that East Clintwood doesn't seem like the place countesses are likely to visit."

Oh how right you are, Twin Whichever--I've lost track.

"Why shouldn't she? She could be visiting John's family."

"But where on earth would they ever meet a countess? We are old money; they're just nouveaux riches."

"Yes, that's a point. Well, let's not worry about it. Even if she's not a countess, our friends will never know, and they'll be impressed when we tell them that we met one."

"Good point, Beatrix."

"Wish I could be a countess--or, even better, a duchess."

"Me too. If we play our cards right, we could probably marry titles. Aristocrats are always looking for money."

"Yes! Oh yes!"

"Maybe she's a countess by marriage."

"Then where was her husband?"

"Could be divorced."

"Or just playing around. Aristocrats are like that."

"That's true. Wish I could find one to play around with."

"So do I, but let's talk about it in the morning. Good night, Yolande."

"Night, Beatrix. Oh--better close the door."

"Yes. And lock it. That way the jewelry will be safe enough until morning when we can return it to the bank vault."

I knew I had to come tonight!

One or other of them switched off the hall lights, though again a little night light glowed. I crept up the remaining stairs to the second floor, waited and listened, and then tiptoed over to the girls' bedroom door. I crouched down and listened carefully. All seemed quiet, but I waited some time to be sure; then taking a thin steel rod from my utility belt--you had a good idea there, Batman--and, with one ear cocked for noises on the stairs or elsewhere in the house, I began to manipulate the key in the lock. Just as I had it in position to push it out onto the floor, I heard a sound on the stairs. Quickly I crossed back to the other side of the hallway, flattened myself against the wall and waited, as in all such circumstances, with bated breath and ready to take action. A maid stepped into the upper hallway. I was just ready to put a hand over her mouth to silence her and render her unconscious with pressure behind the ears when she turned, and walked to a stairway at the other end of the hall, no doubt the access to the servants' quarters. I'm glad I didn't have to take action. She looked like a nice person. Veronica introduced her at this point only to provide a bit of suspense.

I waited to see if anyone would follow her, and when I felt reasonably certain no one would, I returned to the girls' bedroom door. In a trice, before one could say Gaius Julius Caesar Octavianus--I'm also a history buff--I had the key out of the lock, and in a further trice I had the door unlocked. Carefully, silently, I turned the handle. Equally carefully and equally quietly and very slowly, I opened the door a mere crack. I stood for a moment listening. Only the sound of regular breathing. Gently I pushed the door open far enough for me to squeeze through noiselessly and then close it carefully behind me. I felt on the floor for the key and silently returned it to the lock. Then, I felt in my belt for my night goggles.

---Oh good heavens!

I had left them on the kitchen table when I had taken them out to clean! How careless of me! Darn! I'm slipping! good thing I'm getting out of this business. Well, my eyes soon became used to the dark and I tiptoed--not mine Tarquin's ravishing strides (That's from *Macbeth*, in case you're wondering)--over to the elegantly designed twin beds whose outlines I could just see by the dim light through the windows from outside. Beatrix and Yolande--how sweet they looked, the little twits--slept peacefully, innocent of their impending loss, though in what other respects they were innocent I had no idea. Dressers with mirrors--in which my reflection appeared dimly--stood between the beds. From my belt I took my small flashlight--fortunately, it hadn't needed cleaning--with its blue bulb and shone it on the polished marbled tops.

There they were! The emeralds on one and the rubies on the other--or perhaps, because in blue light they both looked black (a fact Veronica remembers from her high school physics) the rubies on one and the emeralds on the other. Anyway, my heart almost skipped a beat--as hearts always do in such circumstances and in this kind of novel--to see before me the prize I had for so long waited! Gloved hands trembling, I reached out to take up a necklace and, shivers running all through me, fastened it about my neck, making doubly sure the clasp was firm. Oh! I could hardly wait to see it in the light! And I could not resist turning a pirouette of delight right there and then. Quietly, of course. Suppressed delight.

But I must get on with the task. Quickly I took up the ear rings and dropped them into a pouch in my belt and tiptoed around to the other dresser for the other set. I stopped in my tracks as the twin whose jewels I had just purloined stirred in her sleep and muttered something about "My Prince!" and clutched her pillow close to her body. Sweet dreams child. Sorry that you will waken to heartache, heartbreak and sorrow. I moved on. As I turned to the other dresser, the other twin stirred in her sleep and muttered something about dwelling in marble halls. (Isn't there an operetta about that somewhere?) Again I froze in my tracks, but she did not waken. I took up the other necklace and earring set--either rubies or emeralds--and again with trembling hands and with shivers running up and down my spine, I wrapped them carefully in kleenex--happily provided by my victim on her bedside table--and dropped them into another pocket of my belt. Then, so happy was I, I clutched my arms about my breasts! But I must not waste time and risk being caught. I tiptoed back to the door, opened it carefully and quietly, listened, peeked out into the hall, and slipped out of the room.

Oh-oh! There came a sound from down the hall. I flattened myself against the wall. (What do you know! Metre and rhyme again! See:

There came a sound from down the hall.

I flattened myself against the wall.)

What if the lights came on? I'd have to take action! But no, nothing. Quickly I crossed the hall to the stairway and began my stealthy descent. But suddenly a light did come on in the upper hall behind me! Reaching the landing, I flattened myself on my lovely flat belly behind the railing and some handy potted palms. Again I prepared myself to take action, hoping I would not have to. I heard a light tapping at the twins' bedroom door.

"Are you all right, girls?" a woman's voice whispered.

After a moment or two a rather sleepy, almost inaudible answer came back, "Nothing's the matter, Mother. We're all right."

"Oh--that's good," said the mother's voice. "I thought I heard something, but I guess not."

In a few moments the light went out. Whew! Another close call. You have good ears, Mother. You should trust them--but I'm glad you didn't. I rose cautiously and completed my descent to the hall. So far, so good, but too many close calls for my liking--though not, of course, for yours, dear Reader. But the work was almost done and my role as Lady Enigma almost played out. Only the painting still to get. And then--then--to reveal myself to Philip and hope that he--!

Just as I was thinking that I was about to get off Scot free, Veronica decided that this time I'd not escape so easily, and that it's time for a little more violent action; and I suppose she's right.

My intention was to use my remote device to reactivate the security system as soon as I was clear of the property, but as I began quietly to unlock the door, I heard a noise behind me. Once again, I ducked into the alcove where the coats were kept. Just as I did, I heard someone say, "Anybody there?"

Then whoever it was, turned on the hall lights.

"Thought I heard something," he muttered.

I'm glad it was a he. I know this is an age of sexual equality, and I'm all for it, but I still have reservations about knocking out, even if need should arise, a she--or should I say a her? Anyway, a woman, a member of my own sex, and John, Veronica's editor--not the disreputable character in the previous chapter--says even a woman attacking a woman is not acceptable nowadays--except of course for such things as Yvette la Flambee's vicious attack in *Romantic Resumes* on Jane Doe which gave Jane the opportunity to demonstrate her new-found self-confidence in self-defence. But I like to immobilize even men as painlessly as possible. After all, I'm not really a vicious person or a man-hater. Of course, when they attack me with tire chains or try to shoot me--but no time for such philosophical niceties at the moment.

I held my breath as the man, the same servant who had tried the door earlier, came down the hall and tried it again.

"Seems okay," he muttered. "Maybe it was outside. Funny. Motion lights should have come on if it were. I'd better--"

I could not let him do whatever it was he had better. In a figurative flash I stepped from between a woman's fur coat and a man's winter jacket and, before the man could turn around and before one could say Karl Ditters von Dittersdorf--again my interest in music--I had pressed my thumb and fourth finger hard on the pressure points behind his ears, and he slumped to the floor. Quickly I drew him back from the door and into the alcove whence I had attacked him, ran and turned off the hall light, found my way to the door using my blue flashlight, opened the door and stepped onto the terrace. In my haste, I made no attempt to relock the door. However, I did use my handy little device to make the the gates swing open for my escape.

Whew! That was close.

Then, just as I thought everything was clear sailing, a pair of headlights swung into the driveway--I had not intended to facilitate such an intrusion--and I had barely time to hit the terrace floor so as not to be caught in their beams.

Now who the heck was this coming home? Do the girls have a brother? Or an older sister?

Whoever he--or she--or it--was, she--or he--or it--was drunk, for the car almost careened over and caromed off one of the great maples in its erratic progress up the driveway, slewed around and came to a screeching, skidding stop facing back to the gate. Perhaps, I thought, I could escape as he--or she--or it--turned the car around again and took it to the garage.

But he, she or it didn't turn the car around or go to the garage. In fact, there were two hes. They got out, singing at the tops of their voices and drunkenly calling for Beatrix and Yolande as they wove their way toward the porch stairs.

They stumbled drunkenly up the stairs and staggered to the door. My lightning quick karate blows--hard enough only to stun--dropped them to the floor. Not even Beatrix and Yolande, the little twits, deserved to have to deal with such louts--just as a window opened upstairs and a male voice called out, "Who's down there? What's going on?"

Quickly I ran to the end of the terrace and vaulted over the wall into the shrubbery below.

I felt my neck. The necklace had a very strong clasp and I had fastened it well; otherwise, I'm sure it would have come off in all this turmoil. I crept from the shrubbery and darted across the lawn to the far side of the yard hoping to be able to get well away in the confusion that was bound to ensue from the discovery of all the inert forms lying in the hall and on the porch. Bent double, I streaked--in the dictionary denotation of the word, not its more recent connotation--among the trees bounding the property and reached the street just as the terrace lights came on an a voice exclaimed, "What on earth has been going on here? Who are these men anyway? Why isn't the security system working?"

Why indeed?

And then I heard a distant shriek: "Oh help! Our jewelry's been stolen!"

I dashed across to the other side of the street and concealed myself behind a tree on the boulevard, and then dodging from tree to tree along the boulevard, I made my way to the end of the street and then walked briskly to my car and got in.

Boy! It's a good thing I am getting out of this business if I'm going to have such close calls as I had tonight. And I've still got to get the painting!

I sank back into the seat a few minutes to catch my breath, then, first making sure no one was around, I turned on the dome light and looked in the rear view mirror to see what I had around my neck.

Rubies!

Appropriate with black! Together with red high heels--but it will be a while before I can wear them publicly. Shucks. Still, despite all the confusion and narrow escapes, I felt very satisfied with myself.

# CHAPTER TEN

I wished I could have worn my rubies with my red belt and high heels when I went to the Gemini Club with Philip on his return, but the theft was too recent and there was too much about the jewels in the news.

When I called for Philip, he was carrying a package, about which he was very mysterious, and stowed it under the seat when he got it.

"A surprise," he said, "for later."

"Oh--Philip!"

When we arrived at the Gemini Club, we walked hand in hand from the car toward the entrance.

Suddenly Philip exclaimed, "Good heavens! I swear I saw a naked woman enter the Club on some guy's arm!"

"What?" I exclaimed. "Darn. I had hoped to be the first to come here nude."

"And I had hoped to be the first to escort you."

"Philip! Really?"

"Yes. I told you I've always had a fantasy of dancing with a naked woman. Shy men have dreams like that. We imagine ourselves great lovers with women falling down at our feet or throwing themselves naked into our arms. But none of that will ever happen us. The world isn't run for shy men. Men are supposed to be aggressive and assertive--macho--and women have been taught that shy men are unmanly; but shy men are very sensual, yet even there our shyness works against us. We go through agonies of emotional turmoil just to ask for a date. And it's no use saying to us, 'Don't worry. The worst she can do is say "No",' because for us that is the worst thing. It says to us we've been rejected. It says to us we're nobodies, that we don't rate with women. A shy man needs a girl--a woman--like you, Stella, to help him overcome his reticence, to lead him gently and patiently into the ability to express his sensual nature, the way you have with me. You've helped me a lot. I don't know why you came to me the way you did that night, but I'll be forever grateful to you for doing so."

"Oh, Philip!"

"In fact, I think it has probably helped me that you've been a woman of mystery more than if I'd known who you are."

"I promise you, Philip, it won't be for much longer. You've been wonderfully patient. I--I have to confess that I went to you initially just on a whim--and because your friends were teasing you so, I felt sorry for you--and because--because I--I like the name Philip--but it didn't take me long to realize that you're a wonderfully sensitive man."

"Actually, it's been kind of fun dating a woman of mystery. And you can do anything you want--cover yourself from head to toe as you are now or be completely naked, you can do or be anything you want, you'll always be aces with me!"

"Philip, you sweetheart," I said and reached up to kiss him. "And you know, I notice you don't stammer now nearly as much as you used to."

"Well, that's your doing too, Stella.

'I never dranke of Aganippe well,

Nor ever did in shade of Tempe sit:

And Muses scorne with vulgar braines to dwell,

Poore Layman I, for sacred rites unfit

Some do I heare of Poets furie tell,

But (God wot) wot not what they meane by it:

And this I sweare by blackest brooke of hell,

I am not pick-purse of anothers wit.

How falles it then, that with so smoothe an ease

My thoughts I speake, and what I speake doth flow

In verse, and that my verse best wits doth please?

Guesse we the cause, What is it thus? fie no;

Or so? much lesse: how then? Sure thus it is:

My lips are sweet, inspired with Stellas kiss.'"

"Oh Philip! You haven't spoken--I mean I haven't heard that since--since I studied it at university!"

He paused, looking off bemused into space for a moment before he said, "Funny, I'm not sure that I ever sat down to memorize it, though I know I've read it. Somehow it just sort of all came back." He shook his head from side to side before he said, "But here we are. Let's go in."

Jake and Judy at the door were all flustered.

"Completely naked!" said Jake.

"Stark!" responded Judy.

"Absolutely nude," said Jake."

"Not a stitch on her!" said Judy.

"The woman who just came in?" I asked.

"Yes," Judy replied. "Oh--it's the lady covered from head to toe in a black cowl and catsuit--and her friend. Well, this other lady--if you can call her that--was completely uncovered--but--well--uh--I--I guess you'd like to go in. Uh--tickets, Jake."

"Oh--yeah. Uh--sorry," stammered Jake. "We--uh--we're all a-fluster here."

The whole Club, when we entered after Jake and Judy had managed somehow to produce our tickets, was also all a-fluster.

"Stark, raving naked!"

"She was wearing high heeled sandals."

"Oh! How observant!"

"Well, I am an engineer."

"But never mind that. What gall!"

"What breasts!"

"What a body!"

"Fred!"

Breasts? Body? Imogen Edwards? Could she be the one? I'd seen her only a few nights ago and knew that she has great breasts and a great body. It's well known around town that she's Manfred Andreotti's woman. Would he demand that--? Or was it her own idea? Would she dare?

And if it is Imogen Edwards, I'm glad I did not come nude tonight. I couldn't stand the comparison--and that raises a real literary problem. As I've said, I'm the heroine of this novel, and heroines are always beautiful, but can every one of us be the most beautiful woman in the world? Some of us must be more beautiful than others, and, well, beautiful though I am, Imogen Edwards is more beautiful. Darn you Veronica! Why did you have to introduce her into my novel? I suppose I should not complain too much. During most of the plot I have been the most beautiful woman in the story--and, if I do say so myself, I stack up pretty favorably. Still, I wish, Veronica, you didn't have this compulsion for intertextuality.

"I wonder who it could be?" said Philip, interrupting my jealous musings.

"I think I've an idea," I said, "but I imagine we'll soon know for certain. What would you like to do, Philip, until the music starts and we can dance?"

"Perhaps we could play Blackjack again."

"You are feeling lucky?" I asked.

"Ra-ther."

"A very British way of putting it."

"I suppose it is--yes. It just came out. I doubt, though, it would have been Sir Philip's way in the sixteenth century. It's more nineteenth, early twentieth century."

"No doubt you picked it up from your reading."

"Probably. Or from watching British movies on television."

During the foregoing chit-chat--not as meaningless as it seems--we reached the cashier's window and bought our chips and then proceeded to the Blackjack table. We both played very cautiously for the first four plays, Philip apparently heeding my advice not to overdo things. But suddenly, on receiving his first card for the fifth play and the dealer's calling for ten dollar bets, he laid ten ten dollar chips on the table.

"Philip!" I exclaimed.

"Don't worry," he said. "I can afford it. By my aunt's will I am suddenly a quite wealthy man. It turns out I was her favorite nephew, and she left the bulk of her estate to me. I'll be able to go to university and take my degree in English after all."

"Oh Philip! That's wonderful--but don't throw your fortune all away at the Blackjack table!"

"Oh don't worry. But as I said, I feel lucky. And look!" he said exposing his cards after the second had been dealt, "A natural!"

"Oh golly Philip!" was all I could say.

When the dealer had paid up, Philip said, "Well, as you wisely advised me, I shall quit while I'm ahead. You see, I'm not being spendthrift and reckless."

When we had cashed--my own winnings were modest--the music began and Philip led me onto the floor to dance. From all sides came the exclamation, "She's going to dance! The naked woman is getting up to dance!"

We turned to look where everyone's eyes were turned and sure enough, a woman completely nude was walking onto the floor with a man in a tuxedo. On seeing her clearly I knew that she was Imogen Edwards. My goodness! What strange contradictions the woman displayed! A couple of weeks ago she was playing classical piano as accompanist to Susan Van Alstyne and now here she is nude on the dance floor of a sleazy night club! And she had stolen a march on me! I wanted to set the ultimate standard in sleaze!

"Let's dance over that way," I said to Philip, nodding in the direction of the nude woman and her escort. "Will you be embarrassed?"

"A little, I guess, but I'll manage."

"You have overcome a lot of your shyness, Philip."

"As I said, thanks to you, Stella."

Now Veronica has asked me to mention that the next couple of pages are taken, with permission, substantially from her editor John Marriott's novel *The Masks of Imogen*--available in paperback from book racks in drug and grocery stores, news stands, bus stations and airports. (This sort of thing is known as intertextuality, by the way.) The only major difference is that here the first person narrative point of view is substituted for the third person point of view.

"Well," I said when we had danced over to the nude woman and her partner, "you and I are the exact opposite."

She turned, as Philip and I danced near to her, to look at me clad from crown to toe in my black cat suit, black gloves and black cowl completely concealing my head and face except for my lovely blue eyes and full, sensual red lips, the blackness of my ensemble dramatically offset by my red high heels and my wide red belt hanging over my hips.

"Why--yes we are," said the woman. "Didn't I see you outside as we came in?"

"You may have, but we sure noticed you!"

"Well, your appearance is quite striking."

"Not nearly as striking as you," I said. "You're spectacular! Actually, I've rather hoped to come here nude myself some day."

"Good for you! You see, Manfred," she said turning to her partner, "I'm not the only one with naughty notions. But why have you come in an all-concealing cowl?"

"Oh, I like being a woman of mystery."

"Stella's a woman of great mystery," said Philip.

Poor Philip. I do feel badly about not letting him see what I look like--for keeping him in such suspense, especially when he puts up with it with such patience.

"Oh!" said the nude Imogen Edwards, to resume the narrative. "Your mysterious friend is called Stella."

"That's what I call her. You see, I'm Philip Sidney. Perhaps, though, you don't understand the allusion?"

"Oh, yes. I understand," replied Imogen. "I'm an English major. So, you're Astrophil and Stella! Wonderful!"

"Yes, that's us," I said. "And you called your friend Manfred--Manfred Andreotti, I suspect. So you are Imogen Edwards."

"Right on both counts," said Imogen. "You see, Manfred, everyone knows who I am."

"But you," said Manfred Andreotti, staring me straight in the eye, "I bet I know who you are."

"Oh! Oh--you--you do?" I exclaimed, quite taken aback, and feeling quite distressed. Was he going to expose my calling to Philip before I did!

"Not your name" said Manfred, "but I know what you are. I won't embarrass you in front of your boy friend, though."

"I rather think the damage has already been done, Manfred," said Imogen Edwards. Despite her brazenness in appearing publicly nude, she seemed a sensitive person. How she could later become--but read *The Masks of Imogen* to find out what she became. "I think you have embarrassed her," she continued, "and unsettled Philip."

"Huh?" grunted Manfred Andreotti.

"You've put questions in his mind."

"Well," I said in a trembling voice but putting up as bold a front as I could manage, "not to worry. It's time Philip knew the truth about me. When we're back at our table Philip," I said, turning to him, "I'll tell you what I've always meant to tell you when the time was ripe, and I guess the time's ripe now."

"Gee, Stella. Whatever it is, it won't make any difference to me."

"Oh, I hope not, Philip! I really hope not. Nice meeting you Imogen-- and you, too, Mr. Andreotti. And don't worry. In some ways you've simply made things easier for me by forcing the issue. Come on, Philip."

I led him by the hand back to our table. We sat down facing each other. Then I lowered my eyes.

"Oh Philip!" I cried, burying my masked face in my gloved hands.

"Please, Stella. It's all right," he said, reaching across and placing his hand reassuringly on my arm. "As I said, I love you, and nothing will change that. But what did Andreotti mean when he said he knew who--or what--you are."

"Philip," I began hesitantly as I looked up again and Philip took both my hands in his, "this costume of mine--except for the high heels and the belt--it--it's my work clothes."

"Your--your work clothes!" he exclaimed, starting back.

"Yes, you see--Oh! Oh dear, oh dear! Oh Philip! This is harder than I thought it would be."

"Please Stella," he said leaning forward again, "you can tell me. But take your time."

"I'm a cat burglar!" I blurted out.

He started and at stared me, mouth open in stunned silence for several seconds.

"A--a cat burglar!"

"Yes," I said meekly. "Now you know. I--I suppose this means it's over between us, Philip."

He was silent again for some moments, seeming to search with in himself.

"Oh no, Stella. No" he said at last and gave my hands a squeeze. "As I said, I love you. You've done too much for me to leave you. But--"

"But what of our future together?" I asked.

"Yes--something like that. Not that I'd--but do you intend to--?"

"I intend to quit--to give it all up after one last escapade to get a painting whose owners have no appreciation of it. Oh! Oh! I know, Philip! It's all wrong, and I should not be involving you in--"

"I am involved, Stella, very deeply involved with you."

"Oh Philip! Cat burgling's in my blood, you see." (Oh, I know, Reader, the inheritance of acquired characteristics is not a biologically sound doctrine, but it happens all the time in fiction.) "I come by it honestly--except, of course, that it's not honest. You see, my father was a cat burglar too."

"Your father was also a cat burglar?"

"Not while he was my father. It was when he knew he was going to be my father that he decided to give it up. And now--largely because I've met you, Philip--Oh! it was something I've intended to do eventually, because you see, it's not something I do because I have to; I've been left very well off and with an interest in the business my father set up; so it's sort of a hobby, you might say--but--but now that I've met you, I--"

I'm not one to give way to emotion, but suddenly I burst out crying again.

"Stella! Stella!" he said and pressed both my hands tenderly in his.

"Oh Philip! How can you still care for me when--?"

"Part of why I like you, Stella, is that you've brought excitement into my life, and what could be more exciting to be in love with a cat burglar?"

"It's partly--largely--for excitement that I became one, Philip," I said looking up and wiping my eyes with my gloved hand. "But some day it's all bound to backfire on me--and of course, now that you know, you should turn me over to the police."

"I'd never do that, Stella."

"As a law abiding citizen you should."

"I suppose so--but I won't. I won't turn in the woman I love!"

"Oh Philip!" I cried. "I don't deserve you!"

"Oh don't start on that line! You remember what Hamlet said about that."

"You mean, 'Treat a man as he deserves and who shall 'scape whipping'?"

"That's the passage."

"Still, I am a criminal."

"Enough! No more of that. I love you, Stella. Do you love me?"

"Oh Philip! Yes! I never knew I could love anyone as much as I love you!"

"Then that's all that matters. I think we should go and make love."

"Oh Philip!"

I know I keep repeating "Oh Philip!" over an over again and that such expressions are trite and become monotonous, but really, it is heartfelt, and some times the fulness of one's heart can be expressed only in the simplest way. So I hope you'll forgive the monotonous repetition. Anyway, what would you say if you were me--I mean "I"--and in similar circumstances?

So we left the Club to deal with Imogen Edwards and her nudity as best it could without us and went to my car. When we got in he leaned over and kissed me.

"Philip! Philip, darling! You are such a wonderful man!"

"And you're a wonderful woman, Stella dearest."

"Would you like to see where I live, Philip?" I asked.

"I'd like that very much, Stella," he replied.

"On the way, I'll tell my story."

"And I'd like to hear it."

"Well," I said as we drove of, "as I've already told you, my father had been a cat burglar, first in England, and then, when the situation was getting too hot for him over there, he came here and took up his trade in New York where he met my mother. And when she became pregnant with me, he did the right thing and married her and moved to East Clintwood and set up as a locksmith. After all, no one could know more about locks than a cat burglar."

"No, I imagine not."

"He was a good father--very fond of me and perhaps a little bit over indulgent, but my mother kept him from going too far. She was in many ways the hard-headed member of the family--though not hard-hearted. Anyway, one day, when I was playing in the attic, I came across Daddy's cat burglar tools. Later when we were alone, I asked him what they were. At first he was hesitant to tell me, but I persisted, and finally he told me his whole story, greatly enjoying doing so, for catburgling was where his heart really was, and as he talked, I realized that that's where my heart was too. That's what I meant when I said I came to it honestly--so to speak--that it's in my blood. I kept asking Daddy how everything worked and how he went about everything. He told me--and was happy to do so--and I was a very good pupil. And then, after he and Mama died, I decided to take up catburgling myself--actually, I'd sort of decided even before that--just for fun--for excitement. And it has been exciting. And that's about it."

"What an amazing story, Stella. And if you hadn't taken it up, maybe you and I would never have met."

"Oh yes! That's true Philip! Then--then you're not upset?"

"How could I be? Your story just makes you that much more fascinating. I'm staid and dull by comparison."

"I don't think you're staid and dull, Philip. You just needed a bit of bringing out."

"And you've done that for me, Stella."

"Oh, you give me far too much credit, Philip. But here we are," I said as I turned into the lane that led to the driveway at the back of my townhouse. When I had pulled to a stop, Philip turned to me, took me into his arms, and kissed me hard, warm, passionately, lovingly--almost as though we were in a Harlequin Romance rather than a playful and trashy novel. But then I suppose this is a bit of a romance novel.

"Oh Philip!" I said. "It's time I removed this cowl and let you see what I look like. You've been so patient--but I guess now you understand why I've kept you in the dark for so long."

"Ah, but I've had your eyes and your lips to nourish my
love--
'Faire yes, sweet lips, deare heart--':
'O eyes, which do the Spheares of beautie move,
Whose beames be joyes, whose joyes all vertues be,
Who while they make Love conquer, conquer Love,
The schooles where Venus hath learned Chastitie.
O eyes, where humble lookes most glorious prove,
Only lov'd Tyrants, just in cruelty,
Do not, o do not from poore me remove,
Keepe still my Zenith, ever shine on me.
For though I never see them, but straight wayes
My life forgets to nourish languished sprites;
Yet still on me, o eyes, dart down your rayes:

And if from Majestie of sacred lights,

Oppressing mortall sense, my death proceed,

Wrackes triumphs be, which Love (high set) doth breed.'

'O kisse, which doth those ruddie gemmmes impart

Or gemmes, or frutes of new-found Paradise,

Breathing all blisse and sweetning to the heart,

Teaching dumb lips a nobler exercise.

O kisse, which soules together ties

By linkes of Love, and only Natures art:

How faine would I paint thee to all mens eyes

Or of thy gifts at least shade out some part.

But she forbids, with blushing words, she sayes,

She builds her fame on higher seated praise:

But my heart burns, I cannot silent be.

Then since (dear life) you faine would have me peace,

And I, mad with delight, want wit to cease,

Stop thou my mouth with still still kissing me.'"

"Oh Philip!" I exclaimed as I stopped his mouth with still fair kissing him. "You wrote the nicest things, and I can certainly fulfil the desire of that last line at least!"

"I wrote the nicest things?" he exclaimed in surprise as our lips parted. "Sir Philip Sidney wrote that!"

"In your earlier incarnation, of course," I said. "You *are* Sir Philip Sidney."

"Yes--Ha! ha!"

But he screwed up his face in a look of deep puzzlement and perplexity even as he laughed--not very convincingly.

From inside the house, Astarte now barked a welcome.

"I think Astarte wants us to go in, Philip," I said.

"Yes," he said, and as we got out of the car, he drew from under the front seat the parcel he had deposited there when we left his place for the Gemini Club earlier in the evening.

"Almost time for my surprise," he said.

We entered, and after Astarte had jumped all over us, almost as happy to see Philip as to see me, I stood gazing at Philip, but as I reached up to remove my cowl he prevented me, saying, "Not yet, Penelope."

"P--P--Pe--Pe--Pen--Pen--Penelope!" I exclaimed. "Oh Philip! How long have you known!"

"Well, I've suspected for some time, but I wasn't quite sure until this evening."

"And--and what happened tonight that made you certain?" I asked.

"Well, your talk just now of my previous incarnation, and before that you're telling me your father was a locksmith. He was more than a locksmith--or he became more than a locksmith. He founded Devereux Security, didn't he? And you're Penelope Devereux."

Do you remember, Reader, that back in CHAPTER TWO I told Max the fence that he should get a system from Devereux Security? That was a clue! You see, by my father's will I'm the owner and honorary president. Now you understand why I--Lady Enigma--Stella--Penelope Devereux-- know so much about security systems and find it so easy to break into the most elaborately protected homes. "Philip darling!" I cried, to return to the main action of the novel and throwing myself into his arms. "Why has it taken so long?"

"It hasn't been very long since we met, Stella--Penelope," he said, his brow furrowed in some puzzlement.

"That's not what I mean, Philip. Why has it taken so many lifetimes."

"So many lifetimes--?" He hesitated a moment in some confusion, and then, so it appeared, the light dawned on him. "Oh! Oh--yes! Yes! Of course! Now I understand! All those strange feelings of *deja vue!* It's not just coincidence of names! And no wonder I so readily remembered those sonnets! I wrote them! Yes--yes, I am Philip Sidney and you are Penelope Devereux from the time of Queen Elizabeth I! We knew and we had known loved each other before!"

"Yes, Philip! Yes! Oh! Why has it taken so so many reincarnations?"

"I--I don't know, Penelope. Who can understand such things? But oh! Why in those days was I so slow to realize I loved you until it was too late and you were Lady Rich!"

"And you, too, were married, Philip, remember."

"Oh, I know. I know. It was a Courtly Love situation."

"And oh Philip! I was tempted, I was tempted. But it doesn't matter any more! The important thing is that we are together at last."

"Oh yes, Penelope! Oh yes! That's all that matters."

"So now I must unmask for you!"

"No, not quite yet either." He drew from the bag he had brought from the car a beautifully gift-wrapped parcel and handed it to me. "For you, Penelope," he said.

I read the card. "To Stella from Astrophil--To Penelope from Philip."

"Wh--what is it, Philip?"

"Open it and see."

I did--eagerly. A pair of blue high heeled shoes with a matching blue hand bag--and what was that I felt inside the hand bag? I opened it to find a blue sequined eye mask.

"I don't need this any more, Philip."

"Just once more, Penelope. But there's something else in there."

"Oh! So there is!"

I took out the velvet covered box and opened it.

"Philip! Sapphires! A necklace and ear rings! But they must have cost you--!"

"I told you, my aunt left me a very considerable fortune."

"Oh Philip! You shouldn't feel you have to spend it all on me."

"I wanted to, Penelope."

"But how did you know my shoe size?"

"I took a peek at a pair in your closet at your cottage while you were busy making breakfast the morning after we made love."

"And why blue? Uh--I don't mean I don't like them in that color."

"To go with the sapphires which go with your lovely blue eyes."

"Oh Philip!"

And once again he burst into poetry:

> "'Ye tradefull Merchants that with weary toyle
> Do seeke most pretious things to make your gain:
> And bothe the Indias of their treasures spoile,
> What needeth you to seeke so farre in vaine?
> For loe my love doth in her selfe containe
> All this worlds riches that may farre be found,
> If Saphyres, loe her eies be Saphyres plaine,
> If Rubies, loe hir lips be Rubies sound:
> If Pearles, hir teeth be pearles both pure and round;
> If Yvorie, her forhead yvory weene;
> If Gold, her locks are finest gold on ground;
> If silver, her faire hands are silver sheene.
> But that which fairest is, but few behold,
> Her mind adornd with vertues manifold."

"But Philip," I said, "that's Edmund Spenser!"

"I know, and even if that was the sonnet Shakespeare was lampooning in 'My Mistress' eyes are nothing like the sun,' Spenser was still a great poet. And what he says is appropriate."

"But my hair's not gold, it's auburn."

"Red gold."

"And I've been a cat burglar, so how can my mind be adorned with virtues?"

"A minor aberration. In all other things you qualify."

"Oh Philip! You say the most beautiful things! And they're all--everything is--just lovely, Philip! I--I'll go upstairs and put them on."

"Don't bother with anything else."

"Philip!" I called back to him as I ran up the stairs. "You naughty boy!"

"It is our intention to make love, isn't it?"

It didn't take long to slip out of my cat suit, to slip my feet into the shoes, fasten the sapphires to my ears and about my neck and, simply because it was part of his gift, slip my arm through the strap of the shoulder bag, and, as he seemed to wish, put on the little blue eye mask, or loup. I walked down the hall and stood for a moment at the head of the stairs while he looked up at me, and then slowly, a step at at time, I descended to him.

He rose from the chair where he had seated himself and spoke:

"'She comes, and streight therewith her shining twins do
move
Their rayes to me, who in her tedious absence lay
Benighted on cold wo, but now appeares my day,
The onely light of joy, the onelie warmth of Love.
She comes with light and warmth, which like Aurora
prove
Of gentle force, so that mine eyes dare gladly play
With such a rosie morne, whose beams most freshly gay
Scortch not, but onelie do darke chilling sprites remove.

But lo, while I do speake, it groweth noone with me,

Her flamie glistring eyes increase with time and place;

My heart cries ah, it burnes, mine eyes now dazled be:

No wind, no shade can coole, what helpe then in my case,

But with short breath, long lookes, staid feet and walking hed,

Pray that my sunne go downe with meeker beames to bed.'"

He advanced to meet me at the foot of the stairs as I descended.

"You're beautiful, Penelope," he said as he took me in his arms.

"Take off my mask first before you say that, Philip."

"I will, but I've always believed you were beautiful," he said as he unmasked me, "and I was not mistaken. You're exactly as I pictured you."

"Oh Philip? Really? How...?"

"Well, I had a little help. That was you at the Symphony, wasn't it?"

"Yes, Philip, but--but how did you know?"

"I didn't right away. It slowly dawned on me afterwards."

"But--but--

"Well, I knew from our second night together that you had auburn hair, and so in my mind's eye I just removed your blond wig and put auburn hair in its place. And now, it's time to make love."

He lifted me into his arms and carried me upstairs.

"Oh Philip! You're so strong!" I said.

"And you're so very beautiful, Penelope," he said as gently he laid me on the bed and lay down beside me and began caressing me.

"My breasts aren't as spectacular as Imogen Edwards's," I said.

"What does that matter, Penelope?" he said, "They're your breasts."

"Philip! You do say the most beautiful things!" And then he said an even more beautiful thing:

"'O joy, too high for my low stile to show:
O blisse, fit for a nobler state then me:
Envie, put out thine eyes, least thou do see
What oceans of delight in me do flow.
My friend, that oft saw through all maskes my wo,
Come, come, and let me powre my selfe on thee;
Gone is the winter of my miserie,
My spring appeares, o see what here doth grow.
For Stella hath with words where faith doth shine,
Of her high heart giv'n me the monarchie:
I, I, o I may say, that she is mine.
And though she give but thus conditionly
This realme of blisse, while vertues course I take,
No kinges be crown'd but they some covenants make.'"

"I don't give myself conditionally this time, Philip," I said, throwing my arms around him and drawing him to me.

Kinky sex is not my thing, but this time, because his gift meant so much to me, I wore the blue high heels he had bought me and, of course, the sapphires.

About a week later Philip escorted me nude on three separate evenings to the Gemini Club. The first time I went in a black wig, red mask and red high heels and Yolande's--or perhaps Beatrix's--rubies, the second time in a blond wig, green mask, green high heels and Beatrix's--or perhaps Yolande's--emeralds, and the third time, the best time of all because I went without any wig but just my own auburn hair--which I'm letting grow out to fall in long voluptuous tresses to my shoulders--and, most important, the blue mask and blue high heels and blue shoulder bag and, about my slender neck and on my ears, the sapphires Philip had given me. Of course I caused a sensation, but one dimmed a bit by Imogen Edwards's earlier appearance. Some guy in the crowd said, "Gosh sooner or later every dame'll be coming naked," but his female companion responded, "Only if we could all look like that." As I said, I'm the heroine, so I do look like that--not quite as like that as Imogen Edwards--but more like that than most--though someone did have to comment, "She hasn't got hooters like that other babe who was here a few nights ago!" Still, it was fun--though by the third time, the sensation had diminished, someone saying when we entered, "Oh, her again." But that's about all I'll tell you about those episodes, for with all that you see on television and in the movies these days, nudity's no longer all that sensational or shocking.

Reader, I married him. Philip wanted me to be married in my cat burglar costume, and I thought of being married in the nude in the back yard of my townhouse, but in the end we decided to be traditional. And I wore my blue high heels and sapphires as my "something blue" at our wedding. After loving him for all those centuries, what else should I have done?

No doubt, Reader, you think that a novel about a heroine who gets away with criminal conduct and in the process meets a nice young man whom she marries and lives with happily ever after is, if not an outright immoral one, then certainly a very amoral one. Well, you're probably right. But as Wendy Steiner said in relation to her book *The Scandal of Pleasure*--I heard her interviewed on the International Service of the Canadian Broadcasting Corporation--literature provides us with an opportunity "to entertain and idea without seeing it as a call to action." After all, the audience does not go out after a performance of *King Lear* and gouge out the eyes of the first people they come across. And besides, this is, after all, a novel playful and trashy. Veronica does not pretend for a moment that what she writes is literature. Her novels would never find their way onto a University English course. But then, that's probably just as well, for if they were so to find their way there, they would become, in Mark Twain's definition, classics, books which everyone wants to have read but no one wants to read. That would be their kiss of death. No doubt, though, someone will make Veronica's novels the subject of a doctoral dissertation--"The Symbolism of Masks and High Heels in the Trashy Fiction of Veronica Verity," or some such title. But there is no symbolism. Veronica simply likes masked heroines in high heels because she thinks they make us look sexy--which they do, and we are--but stupider subjects have been chosen for those weighty studies that sit on university library shelves collecting dust while the paper disintegrates.

After I had sent out notices to all my clients indicating that *la Comtesse Madeleine de la Fontaine* was returning to France to reclaim her inheritance, I did go back to steal the painting--the *Troisieme Étude* of Charles Camille Duparc--sort of as a wedding present for Philip, though I did buy him something too. Since the painting's original owners had hung it upside down, I felt it should be housed properly, and I did replace it--upside down--with the very good reproduction made by Gordon Clark and Glen Campbell, fakers, forgers and fabricators extraordinary. No one will ever know the difference--certainly not its original owners!

I don't know whether the Vanderhafen twins ever tried to look up la Comtesse de la Fontaine when they visited France or what they would have thought when they were told that the la Fontaine line had died out and there was no such person. However, I did return their emeralds and rubies by courier from Winnipeg, Manitoba--giving totally fabricated return address: the name of a family in East Kildonan as living at a house and street in St. Boniface. After Philip's gift of sapphires, they no longer had any meaning for me. And after all, though the poem says nothing about emeralds, Philip said (quoting Spenser) that my lips are rubies. And besides, as I've said, the real satisfaction was in the theft and in the wearing of them when I went nude to the Gemini Club, not in owning them.

Why Winnipeg, you may ask? Well, Philip and I both decided to study English, and we were accepted to do so at the vast, intimidating, intellectually over-sophisticated but lushly lovely campus of the University of British Columbia in the sprawling, worldly-wise and just plain worldly, somewhat decadent, perhaps even slightly wicked but rather exciting and certainly gorgeously situated West Coast Canadian city of Vancouver--or so lovely young Jane Doe--another utterly gorgeous romantic heroine-- perceived them in Veronica's novel *Romantic Resumes*--though why, you may ask, after what I said above about doctoral dissertations I want to do that, I don't know, except that I like to learn--and Winnipeg was on the way. I sold Devereux Security to a consortium, but I hear now that Imogen Edwards--who became Crime Queen of the Clintwoods after Manfred Andreotti's murder--has acquired a controlling interest--as she has in every other business enterprise in the Clintwoods--so she has easy access to just about every home and business in the twin cities, though in fact, she does not need it, for she can get what she wants simply by snapping her fingers, so I hear.

As it turned out, we were fortunate to have left East Clintwood. As Crime Queen, Imogen Edwards, or Miss as she requires everyone to call her, became so iron-fisted as leader of the crime syndicate that her name is more feared than ever the name Andreotti had been--they say she can even intimidate the New Jersey godfather--and whereas Manfred Andreotti had left alone the small-time crooks like Lady Enigma to pursue their felonious little plans unmolested so long as they didn't encroach on what he considered his domain, Imogen has tracked them all down and made them pay her for the privilege of being allowed to operate.

As we traveled, with Astarte in the back seat, across the free open clean and innocent Canadian Prairies--home of the aforementioned lovely young

Jane Doe--we frequently listened to the car radio. One day near Moose Jaw, Saskatchewan, when we returned to the car after stopping for lunch and letting Astarte have a run, I turned on the radio and recognized the music.

"Oh Darling!" I exclaimed to Philip, who was driving. "They're playing our song!"

"Wha--? Oh yes!" he replied. "Mahler's Tenth Symphony in the Revised Deryck Cooke Performing Version! Lovely, isn't it!"

When we were settled into the house we bought in Vancouver, we hung the *Troisieme Étude* of Charles Camille Duparc where we hoped few would see it in the master bedroom. Philip suggested we admit it was the real one and that the *Quatrieme Étude*, which was simply the Troisieme upside down, hung in a private residence in East Clintwood, but I thought that might create suspicion, and so when anyone did see it and ask about it, we decided to follow Holy Writ where we find--if one resorts to a little jiggery-pokery--that "A lie is abomination unto the Lord...and a very present help in time of trouble" and said it was a copy--a very good one.

At the University of British Columbia, we were soon dubbed Astrophil and Stella by everyone in the English Department who all wondered how we had come to meet and whether we were in any way connected with the two illustrious Elizabethans. "We met purely by chance at a dance once," said Philip, "and, as a matter of fact, we are the reincarnations of the Elizabethan Penelope Devereux and Philip Sidney."

Everyone, of course, laughed and forgot the whole matter forthwith. While on some occasions, a lie, even though an abomination unto the Lord, may indeed be a very present help in time of trouble, at other times truth is the best defence.

Our first year corresponded to the final year of Manuel Fernando de Ortega y Diaz de Rodriguez, Duque de Pontevedra y Alicante, and his lovely young Duquesa, Juana Marguerita de Doe y Ortega y Diaz de Rodriguez, the aforesaid former equally lovely young Jane Margaret Doe and whose story, as noted, you can read in Veronica's novel *Romantic Resumes*. We got to know them quite well, and we still keep in touch, for they are a lovely couple.

I've kept my cat burglar costume--not for the purpose of renewing my former career, but because Philip wanted me to. He likes me to wear it with my red belt and red high heels in the evenings sometimes when, after setting aside our studies, as a reminder of how we first met, we dance in our living room to Strauss Waltzes on CDs. I also wore it once to a Hallowe'en dance, and of course, everyone thought I had come disguised as Michelle Pfeiffer playing Catwoman. As I pointed out to you in the first chapter of this *romanza giocoso e cianfrusaglioso,* I pointed out to them that my costume has no ears and the cowl covered my whole face.

Well, there's not much else to tell you except that Philip and I are very happy. My only worry is that Charles Blount, Eighth Baron Mountjoy, my second love, may have been reincarnated somewhere. That could cause problems!

# AUTHOR BIOGRAPHY

Veronica Verity is the nom de plume of John Eric Marriot, born in Saskatoon, Saskatchewan, in 1931. He obtained his PhD in English from the University of British Columbia in 1994. He currently lives in Vancouver, British Columbia.